"**H**ello there, Dirk," her voice faded as she stared at the man before her. She was shocked on so many levels. This guy before her was not Dirk James; he was Lance Cauldwell, her first love. She knew every line of that face. She had once tried to count every one of his thick, stubby eyelashes.

He looked the same—no better, way better. She saw why Alex was gushing over him; she had done the same when she was seventeen, and he was their next-door neighbor studying for his master's at the university.

"Lance!" Cayenne hissed, "When did you change your name to Dirk?"

"Excuse me?" the guy in front of her stepped back. He looked at her with no recognition behind his eyes. "It seems as if I have the wrong address!"

"No er…sorry," Cayenne stammered. She was confused. Was he Lance Cauldwell's twin or something? He obviously did not know who she was.

"My name is Cayenne," she cleared her throat, "Alex sent me to greet you; she went to freshen up."

"Oh, nice to meet you, Cayenne," he held his hand out for her to shake, and when Cayenne put her hand in his, all the hairs on her arm stood on end.

CAYENNE

BRENDA BARRETT

CAYENNE
A Jamaica Treasures Book/November2024
Published by Jamaica Treasures
Manchester, Jamaica

This is a work of fiction. Names, characters, places, and incidents are either the product of the author's imagination or are used fictitiously. Any resemblance to an actual person or persons, living or dead, events, or locales is entirely coincidental.

ISBN 978-976-97430-1-4

ALSO BY BRENDA BARRETT

FULL CIRCLE
NEW BEGINNINGS
THE PREACHER AND THE PROSTITUTE
AFTER THE END
THE EMPTY HAMMOCK
THE PULL OF FREEDOM
REBOUND SERIES
THREE RIVERS SERIES
NEW SONG SERIES
BANCROFT SERIES
MAGNOLIA SISTERS SERIES
SCARLETT SERIES
WILEY BROTHERS SERIES
PRYCE SISTERS SERIES
THE JACKSONS SERIES
CRIMSON HILL SERIES
SPICE AND STONE SERIES
RIDGEVIEW SERIES

ABOUT THE AUTHOR

Brenda Barrett is an award-winning and bestselling author who has a passion for writing real Jamaican romances.

When she's not weaving words that transport readers to exotic locales, you can find her nurturing her green thumb in the garden or doting on her beloved cats.

With an infectious zest for life, this author brings a unique perspective to her writing that is both relatable and thought-provoking.

Don't be surprised if you find yourself lost in the pages of her latest work, as she seamlessly blends romance with some drama, mystery, and suspense, or even sci-fi, leaving readers wanting more.

You can connect with Brenda online at:
Brenalbar.com
Twitter.com/AuthorWriterBB
Facebook.com/AuthorBrendaBarrett

Chapter One

"**I** never thought I'd say this," Alex said, plopping herself down on the lounge chair beside Cayenne. "I am in love."

Cayenne snorted. "You say that all the time." She was sipping a welcome drink brought to them by the butler at their villa.

"But this time, I really mean it," Alex said. "I swear, my heart hasn't righted itself from the moment Dirk walked into the office two months ago. Did I describe him to you?"

"Several times," Cayenne said patiently. She felt lightweight and carefree and could listen to Alex wax poetic all day about her co-worker.

The breeze was refreshing, and the scenery was top-tier. Everywhere she looked had blue skies and sea views.

Alex had rented an eight-bedroom villa for the long holiday weekend and had invited a few of her friends and this Dirk fellow, who she was constantly fawning over like a ditzy schoolgirl.

They had found the poolside after they had chosen their rooms, and since then, Dirk was all Alex could talk about.

"He has the aesthetic that I like," Alex said, "mocha-toned skin, thick level brows, dark brown eyes the color of rich mahogany, and juicy pink lips. I can barely concentrate on what he is saying most of the time. When he speaks, a rush of wind starts in my ear, and I only hear him from a distance. I see his lips, though; they move in slow motion."

"Isn't that a bad thing?" Cayenne asked, concerned. "You just got promoted; you can't afford to zone out of hearing your colleagues, no matter how delicious they look."

"I know," Alex said, unconcerned. "But I can't help it."

Cayenne adjusted her sunglasses and placed them on top of her hair. No matter how much Alex promoted Dirk, Cayenne didn't like him. He wasn't a part of their friend crowd. Alex had asked him to stay the entire weekend, and they didn't even know him. He would be a cuckoo in the group of twelve, changing the dynamic because Alex would act coquettish and coy around him. Cayenne hated it when Alex went into her sophisticated mode.

It would all be an act for the rest of their time there.

"What time is Dirk coming by?" Cayenne asked lazily.

"Why can't you wait to meet him?"

"No," Cayenne said, "just wondering when you will start putting on your actress persona and start acting weird. As you do around every guy you like at first."

"I don't act weird," Alex sighed, "I do, don't I?"

"Oh yes," Cayenne nodded. "And when the thrill wears off, you start acting normal again, and then you get bored and dump them."

"I don't think I will ever be bored of Dirk James," Alex said dreamily. "When he stepped into the office on his first day, I instantly knew he would change my life. Do you think he'll like it here?"

"Oh, he will," Cayenne nodded. "It's gorgeous, luxurious, and exclusive. What's not to like? You are going all out for this weekend; it must be costing you an arm and a leg."

"It's fine," Alex said breezily.

"I didn't want to say anything," Cayenne said, concerned, "but lately you've been spending recklessly. What about saving up for a house?"

"Relax, young one," Alex laughed, "I know what I am doing. I am the newest senior wealth manager at LAD Wealth Management. I should advise you on money management, not vice versa."

"I know," Cayenne said, "that is why I am concerned. I know how much you earn, and funding your latest lifestyle is not sustainable."

"You know about my base salary," Alex said, "but there are incentives and..." Her phone buzzed. Someone was at the gate.

She grabbed the phone and gasped. "He is here. He is not supposed to be here until twelve like the others. I have to go and get dressed," Alex said, panicking, "you go and greet him. Keep him entertained."

"Okay," Cayenne said, looking down at herself. She and Alex wore identical cute, lightweight dresses that she had picked up at a craft market. She felt peeved that Alex thought the dresses were not presentable enough for her precious Dirk.

"There is nothing wrong with your dress," she pointed to Alex, but her friend was already inside, and running towards her room in a panic.

Cayenne shook her head. She didn't want to move from her sheltered spot overlooking the glistening blue pool, but she had to meet Dirk and keep him entertained per Alex's instructions.

She checked herself in the floor-to-ceiling mirror in the hallway and confirmed that there was nothing wrong with the dress. Her face was okay but she had chewed off all her lip gloss so she refreshed the gloss and headed for the front door. She fixed a welcoming smile on her lips and opened the door.

"Hello there, Dirk," her voice faded as she stared at the man before her. She was shocked on so many levels. This guy before her was not Dirk James; he was Lance Cauldwell, her first love. She knew every line of that face. She had once tried to count every one of his thick, stubby eyelashes.

He looked the same—no better, way better. She saw why Alex was gushing over him; she had done the same when she was seventeen, and he was their next-door neighbor studying for his master's at the university.

"Lance!" Cayenne hissed, "When did you change your name to Dirk?"

"Excuse me?" the guy in front of her stepped back. He looked at her with no recognition behind his eyes. "It seems as if I have the wrong address!"

"No er…sorry," Cayenne stammered. She was confused. Was he Lance Cauldwell's twin or something? He obviously did not know who she was.

"My name is Cayenne," she cleared her throat, "Alex sent me to greet you; she went to freshen up."

"Oh, nice to meet you, Cayenne," he held his hand out for her to shake, and when Cayenne put her hand in his, all the hairs on her arm stood on end.

She hurriedly pulled her hand away and stepped aside for him to pass.

She had only had this reaction to one guy. His name was Lance Cauldwell, and he looked exactly like Dirk James.

Something was not adding up.

"I have no idea which room she had assigned to you because she wasn't sure you would come," Cayenne stammered. "But I am supposed to entertain you until she comes down. Have a seat, please. Make yourself at home, and welcome to Sea Glass Villas."

He looked at her and smiled ruefully, "I came too early, didn't I?"

Cayenne looked at the clock. "You did."

"Sorry about that. I was in the neighborhood; my grandparents have a place close by, so I had to stop by and say hello. Unfortunately, they are visiting Jamaica for a funeral."

"So sorry to hear," Cayenne nodded.

She was staring at him fixatedly. She had to stop. She could see why Alex said she zoned out when he was speaking. She used to do the same thing to Lance when she was seventeen. His lips were a rose-pink hue.

Could two people look exactly alike with the same features, including the same shade of lips?

"Do you have a twin brother?" Cayenne asked curiously.

"No," Dirk said.

"Are you sure?" Cayenne asked.

"Quite sure," Dirk nodded. "My mother would have told me if she had twins."

"Maybe she gave your brother away," Cayenne said, "and kept you."

Dirk laughed. "I doubt it. She loves children. Besides, my grandparents on both sides of the family tree would not have allowed that. I have four siblings."

"Is one of them called Lance?" Cayenne asked.

"No." Dirk shook his head. "They are all younger than I am. My mother found the love of her life eighteen years ago, and they've been busy popping out babies ever since."

Cayenne chuckled. "That sounds like something Lance would say."

"So, he looks like me and has the same sense of humor?"

"That's right." Cayenne nodded. "What about your father? Could you have a sibling called Lance on his side of the family?"

"No," Dirk shook his head. "Unfortunately, I was his only child. He died before I was born in a biking accident while he was on vacation here in Jamaica."

"Oh, sorry to hear." Cayenne looked deflated. "This is a crazy coincidence."

"Who was Lance to you?" Dirk asked.

"My next-door neighbor when I was seventeen," Cayenne said sheepishly. "My first real love. What I felt for him was so pure and, deep and all-encompassing. I vowed that I would never get married if I can't feel for my future husband the way I felt about Lance."

Dirk frowned. "Wow, I assume you are not married now?"

"No," Cayenne chuckled, "but I may have taken that little bit of childish infatuation a bit too far. Maybe seeing you today is a sign that I need to update my vow."

"I hope that's not the case," Dirk said. "Pure, deep, all-encompassing love is something to aspire to. Settling for less will make you and the other person miserable."

"You are right," Cayenne smiled. "You are cool. I see why Alex is so into you."

He smiled, but it didn't reach his eyes. Cayenne noted. He was not that into Alex. So why was he here? And why did the prospect of him not liking her friend give her a little fissure of joy?

Maybe because she was fascinated with Dirk James. He looked and felt like Lance. Her head hadn't worked out the difference yet, but she wouldn't be the kind of friend who would come between her friend and the guy she loved.

"Oh hey, Dirk," Alex came downstairs in a tight blue dress and furry blue house slippers. Her hair, previously in a ponytail, was now down her back in loose waves as if she had used a curling iron.

Her dusky skin was glowing; she had used her no-makeup look, which meant she actually had on makeup, but it looked effortless. She looked like a perfect Barbie doll.

"Hello, Alex," Dirk said. "You look amazing."

"Thank you," Alex sat down. "I am so happy you could make it."

"Me too." Dirk nodded. "I haven't had a vacation on this side of Jamaica in ages."

"Would you like some refreshments?" the butler interrupted any further conversation. He listed the names of the drinks. "Lunch will be served at one o'clock, as agreed, Miss Alex."

Alex nodded. "Thank you, Balfour."

"Cayenne, a moment, please," Alex indicated to the patio. Cayenne got up and followed her.

"Isn't he dreamy?" Alex squealed when they were on the patio.

"Yes, he is," Cayenne said. "You were right; he could be a dead ringer for Lance Cauldwell. I wish you had met him so that you can confirm whether I am hallucinating or not."

Alex looked uninterested in the comparison. "Listen, kiddo, I must ask you to switch rooms. Your room is beside mine, and I want Dirk beside me instead."

"That means I am going to have to share with Sanya," Cayenne said. "She's the only single girl; Anthony and Jerome are going to bunk together, and then the couples will have their rooms."

"Make it happen, love," Alex said excitedly, oblivious to

her displeasure. "Don't be a spoilsport. This is a once-in-a-lifetime opportunity to have Dirk James right where I want him. Besides, I couldn't have him sharing with Sanya, could I?"

"True," Cayenne sighed. "We didn't take that into consideration when you invited him. I hate sharing rooms. Where is the loyalty of sisterhood?"

"I want that man," Alex said. "Sisterhood is taking a back seat this weekend. I am going all out to get him. I still can't believe he came. He didn't show me one lick of interest in the office. You and Sanya better stay in your lane; he is mine."

Cayenne chuckled. "Okay."

Chapter Two

The rest of the crowd came trickling in by noon. Cayenne breathed a sigh of relief. She had seriously felt like a third wheel and was frustrated with how over-the-top Alex was acting. She put on her best lady of the manor voice and glided around the house with Dirk as her captive audience.

It was left up to her to play hostess while Alex ignored the rest of them.

"So that's the latest love of her life," Joey chuckled when Cayenne showed him and Iris to their room. Joey was one of Alex's exes who became a good friend, and Iris, his girlfriend, was Alex's friend from college too.

Most of the group were Alex's friends from college. Only Anthony, Jerome, and Sanya were their mutual friends from high school.

"Yes," Cayenne answered.

"He seems familiar," Joey mused. "Where have I seen him before?"

"You feel that way too?" Cayenne asked.

"Oh yes," Joey nodded.

"He looks exactly like a guy I used to know named Lance Cauldwell," Cayenne said. "Does the name ring a bell?"

"Not sure," Joey frowned. "It will come to me."

"I know where I have seen him before. He models underwear," Iris said. "Wasn't he on the pack of boxers I got for you the other day?"

"No, I don't think so," Joey said. "It could be."

"He is fine," Iris said dreamily. "But not as fine as Joey," she amended when he looked at her sharply.

"Okay, then," Cayenne shook her head. And there I was thinking that you really had seen him somewhere before. I am going to see Kinsley and Tessa to their room. The butler said that lunch would be served at one."

She exited the room and gave Kinsley and Tessa a brief tour, stopping at the room Alex had designated for them.

"Does Dirk look familiar to you?" Cayenne asked Kinsley. He was Alex's cousin and second bestie; he and his wife Tessa had a debt collections business. They were experts at tracking down people. Kinsley, in particular, never forgot a face or a name.

"Mmm," Kinsley said thoughtfully. "Can't say I recognize him from anywhere specific, but he does have that familiar aura about him, doesn't he?"

"He reminds me of that stock photo we used for our advertisement," Tessa said. "You know that photo with the handsome guy posing beside the car."

"Oh yeah," Kinsley nodded. "Yeah. He does resemble him. Was he a model?"

"I don't know," Cayenne shook her head. "He does resemble a neighbor I had a couple of years ago, though."

"People look alike," Tessa yawned. "Listen, Cayenne, all

I am here for this weekend is to sleep. Work is kicking our butts. We are only here because we would be fools to give up on a free vacation in a lovely place."

"With free meals," Kinsley added.

"Free meals," Tessa licked her lips. "When are we going to eat, do you know?"

"Lunch is at one."

"Maybe Kinsley will make it," Tessa said tiredly, curling up on the bed. "Save me something from it, hun," she told her husband.

Cayenne could hear snores before she exited.

Kehlani and Noah were given the last bedroom upstairs. They were hyped to be there, and no, they had never seen Dirk before. Matt and Lacy took one of the two bedrooms downstairs, and Jerome and Anthony shared the other.

Everyone was accounted for. They were a good bunch of people, and as usual, they had a lot of laughs and fun when they hung out.

Cayenne decided to unpack before going downstairs to eat. Her roommate, Sanya, was bubbling over with excitement.

"It's nice here! It makes me want to work harder to afford all of this, like Alex. I love the wraparound patio," she gushed. "Smell that fresh air."

Cayenne smiled. She had been just as enthusiastic when she first arrived.

"I like your dress," Cayenne said.

Sanya grinned. "Thank you! I went shopping at the Salvation Army store, and wouldn't you know it, some fashionista had offloaded a ton of nice, brand-new clothes. I felt bad that I got them so reasonably priced."

"You are still trawling charity shops for clothes," Cayenne chuckled. "I thought that was something you would have outgrown by now."

"It's called thrifting, and I'll never outgrow it. It's fun—my favorite hobby," Sanya shook her head. "I can't understand why more people don't participate in it in Jamaica. Instead of hoarding thousands of shoes and clothes in your closets—some of which you haven't worn—donate them to a thrift shop. Then people like me, who have no qualms about wearing gently used clothes or clothing not worn at all, will buy it, and the proceeds can go to something good. It's good for the environment and good for the budget. Your trash is another man's treasure. And in this case, I bought a suitcase worth of treasure from some charitable fashionista."

Cayenne laughed. "You are preaching to the choir. I raid Cinnamon's closet all the time. Her closet is my thrift store, except unlike you, I don't pay a dime."

"I would do the same thing, except my older sister is much bigger than me. Her clothes are nice but can't fit me. By the way, how is the lovely Cinnamon?" Sanya asked.

"Happy, contented, enjoying life as a stay-at-home mom for now. VJ is going to be a year old in a few weeks."

"Time flies," Sanya nodded. "And how is your mom? Has she changed her name to Greystone yet?"

"Nope." Cayenne shook her head. "She can't be bothered."

Sanya laughed. "You know I like her. She does what she wants to do, and too bad if you don't like it. Does she have a boyfriend yet? Last year, she was on a television morning show bragging that she was celibate for a full year. They gave her a prize."

"I didn't even know about that." Cayenne groaned. "I wish my mother would keep some things private. Is that too much to ask?"

Sanya laughed. "Your mother is an open book; why do you want to close her up? Speaking of Anise, why does she look younger than me? Can you ask her for her skin regimen?"

Sanya peered in the mirror. "My face is looking rough."

"Your face is fine," Cayenne grinned. "You are just fishing for compliments. Your skin is glowing; your face could sell a thousand magazines."

"Just a thousand?" Sanya smirked. "Say, you don't have any of your expensive spa products with you, do you? Maybe I could ramp it up to ten thousand magazines."

"You are incorrigible," Cayenne shook her head. "I carried a package just for you. I know you depend on them for your skin routine."

"Oh, bless you, my friend," Sanya grinned. "I love having rich friends."

"Since when am I a rich friend?" Cayenne raised her eyebrows. "I am a working woman just like you."

"Rich adjacent, then. Some of the blessings are spilling over," Sanya said.

"Rich adjacent?" Cayenne chuckled. "How do you figure that?"

"Your mother is a Greystone, your sister married Jaxon Wilde, and your father was Paul Aubry. Some money has to be in the mix for you."

Cayenne laughed.

"I was surprised that Alex was the one paying for this place. I thought it would have been you. With Anise being part of the one percent, I was waiting for you to start spending some of her cash."

"If my mother were going to start doling out money, she would do it for something serious like a house or a business," Cayenne said, "not for a weekend with my friends. She might look and sound flaky, but Anise is a shrewd businesswoman who raised us to be responsible with our finances. Besides, I am saving to buy a townhouse. The one beside us is for sale. And after I buy it, I will have to do some significant renovations."

Sanya nodded. "Fair enough." She sat down on the opposite bed from Cayenne. "Sounds like you have your wits about you. So tell me, how can Alex even afford this?"

Sanya lowered her voice, "I went searching for this villa when Alex told us to come over for the long weekend, and it costs a whopping $12,000 a night. We'll be here for three nights. And she didn't ask us to chip in."

"Not that I could. I don't even have fifty dollars to rub together. Between student loans, my braces, and my credit card bill, I am perpetually broke. I hitched a ride here with Kinsley and Tessa; my car is acting up again. I am seriously considering dating my mechanic to get free maintenance at this point."

Cayenne laughed. "It can't be that bad."

"Girl, every other month, I am at his shop. He is beginning to look cuter and cuter the more I see him. And as you know, Caleb and I are in no man's land right now, so I am practically single. Not quite, but nearly there."

Cayenne reached for her phone. "Thirty-six thousand US, you said, for three days?"

"Yup." Sanya nodded. "I almost fell out of my chair when I saw what it was going for. Did Alex win the Lotto, and you guys are keeping it secret?"

"No," Cayenne shook her head. "She was promoted to Senior Wealth Manager six months ago. I'm sure you got the message in our friends' group."

"I did," Sanya said, "but that doesn't mean she is suddenly rich. She is making good money, but not 'this villa for three days' kind of money. I work in payroll at the bank and got promoted the other day. I can't tell you specific figures, but none of our wealth managers could afford this place on their salary in one fell swoop. Unless they are rich already. Did

Alex's parents win the lottery?"

Cayenne shook her head. "No. Congrats on getting the promotion, though."

"Thanks, but it's more work than money. They could keep the promotion," Sanya rolled her eyes. "Did that crusty brother of hers finally make anything from his online currency trading?"

"I don't think so," Cayenne was troubled now. She should have been asking these questions in the six months since Alex started living like a rock star.

Her parents weren't rich; they were both middle-class and civil servants. Her mother was an education officer, and her father was a regional director in the Ministry of Health. As for her brother Sebastian, he still lived in his parent's basement apartment where he day traded, hooked on the promise of making a big payout. He had moments where he made money and moments where he lost it all. His moods and hygiene were tied to his trading losses and gains. The last time she saw him, his hair had started to loc, but not in an attractive way, and he had looked and smelled like a homeless person with no access to bathroom facilities. So it stood to reason that he was in a losing cycle.

"I am pretty sure there is a reasonable explanation," Sanya said. "I am just overthinking things. I will turn off my brain, enjoy this weekend to the fullest, and take as many pictures as possible. My Instagram is about to be lit."

"Yup," Cayenne said unenthusiastically. Unfortunately, she didn't have the luxury of turning off her brain. Alex was her best friend, so alarm bells were going off in her head. Hearing the figures so starkly laid out, she wondered how on earth Alex was affording things. She had bought a new car the other day, moved into the Wilde building, and was eating out at high-end restaurants every other night.

Cayenne had unashamedly participated in a few of those dinners.

"So, change of topic." Sanya snapped her fingers. "Tell me about the guy."

"Which guy?" Cayenne asked.

"The pretty guy," Sanya grinned. "You know who I am talking about, the one downstairs who Alex can barely look away from to introduce to us. I don't chat with Alex often enough these days; we are all busy. I didn't know there was a new guy on the scene. What happened to what's his name?"

"Myron," Cayenne chuckled. "He was unceremoniously dumped by text."

"Never liked him," Sanya said.

"Me neither," Cayenne agreed.

"So about this one..." Sanya raised her eyebrows. "What's the tea?"

"He works at LAD Wealth," Cayenne said. "Alex has been crushing on him for two months since he started there. He looks a lot like Lance Cauldwell. Remember him? The guy I used to crush on."

"Ooh, I remember you talking about him nonstop," Sanya said. "He was doing his master's and lived next door, and you were planning your wedding and wondering what your babies would look like."

"That's the guy!" Cayenne nodded. "They look exactly alike. They could be the same person."

"Maybe they are the same person." Sanya wiggled her eyebrows.

"Can you be serious for a moment?" Cayenne said earnestly. "This is baffling. How can two people look exactly alike, speak the same, smile the same, have identical teeth and eyes, and inflections on words, and they are not related?"

"It's a mystery," Sanya said. "But I was standing in Burger King the other day, minding my own business, anticipating my Whopper, when who should I see but my aunt Trudy, my mother's youngest sister, in my favorite blouse, eating alone at the corner of the restaurant. I lost my spot in the line and went over to her, ready to accuse her of wearing out my clothes. But wouldn't you believe it, it wasn't Trudy."

"It wasn't?" Cayenne raised an eyebrow.

"Nope. No ma'am," Sanya said. "She could be a replica for Trudy. I showed her pictures, I grilled her about her family, and she grilled me about mine, but we concluded that we weren't related. They just looked alike, and that's all there was to it."

Cayenne nodded. "Well, what about how I feel? I feel as if he is Lance. I can't explain it."

"You had better lose those feelings fast," Sanya chuckled. "The way I see Alex acting like the sun, moon, and stars rise and set on this guy, if you so much as give him a smile, she'll freak out and cut you off."

"We've been friends too long to have a guy come between us like that," Cayenne snorted.

Sanya laughed and fell over on the bed. "You crack me up, Cayenne. Alex would drop you like she does so many of her boyfriends. They were always the greatest loves until they weren't."

Cayenne shook her head. "I doubt that. But I won't test your theory. I'll stay away from Lance—I mean, Dirk."

"Girl, you are in trouble." Sanya grinned. "This weekend is shaping up to be lit."

Chapter Three

Dirk should award himself a medal; he had acted convincingly all evening, showing interest in Alexandria Hall, but she was a tough nut to crack. All his leading conversations about work, money, and spending were met with deflection after deflection. She was adept at redirecting, but he was tenacious and motivated to crack this case wide open. He would try harder with her.

He had been at this for two months, poring over the figures, combing through them with a fine-toothed comb, applying all his forensic skills to this mystery. Everything looked as it should, but a few things weren't adding up: Alex's sudden wealth and the managing director, Stephen Grant's, new yacht.

It didn't take long for Alex to be on his radar; her spending habits had suddenly increased into the luxury category precisely six months ago. At first, she had been modest with it. One month, she bought herself a new car, which was nothing too flashy, but it was way out of her salary range, and she hadn't gotten a loan. The following month, she paid off her student loans. She moved from her modest one-bedroom apartment to a two-bedroom apartment at the Wilde Building. Her city-view apartment was costly. In fact, that rental was why she was on his radar.

She had also unexpectedly been promoted to senior wealth manager by Stephen Grant himself, bypassing HR and the merit system in place at the company. She was only twenty-three and had worked at the company for two years. According to HR records, her work had not been exceptional. She wasn't in the pipeline for a promotion, which led him to believe that Stephen Grant was involved in whatever scheme they had going on. He needed Alex to be a senior wealth manager to handle a big account.

He intended to find out what that scheme was and if it involved any of LAD Wealth's client accounts. He needed Alex to point him in the right direction. He would shadow her closely this weekend, listen to her every word, and gather clues. When people were at their most relaxed, they usually gave themselves away.

He was quite happy that she had developed a romantic interest in him and had invited him on her long weekend break. This was the perfect opportunity to have a breakthrough in the case. But he had not foreseen the Cayenne Aubry angle. She had recognized him instantly and almost blew his cover.

Through the years, he had thought about her on and off. He had speculated about where she was but always held back from contacting her. She had been a special girl, but they couldn't have had a relationship then. He had been sorely tempted but had been four years older at twenty-one and focused on accomplishing his goals. He had a late start in life because of his maternal grandparents, Daphne and

Joshua Cauldwell. They lived a few miles from where he was now in the hills of St. Mary.

When he was five, his mother left him with his grandparents to work as a babysitter for a wealthy family in Cayman. His grandparents held him back from school after she left and used him as their farmhand for years. He had an aunt and an uncle who were also farmers living nearby, they sent their children to school and unsuccessfully pleaded with their parents to send him. However, it was useless; they liked the free labor too much.

His grandfather did not see the value in education, as he couldn't read or write. His grandmother had a basic education did whatever her husband said. They needed help on their small dairy farm, where they also sold eggs. They spent the money his mother sent for school supplies to expand their farming operation instead. Dirk's job was to milk the cow in the mornings and collect the eggs. In the midday, he would help his grandfather in the vegetable patch. He used to sit and watch his cousins going to school longingly.

Then, his mother's oldest sister, Verona, the first of the family to have left the district and the country, came to visit one summer. She was a nurse in the US but had been injured on the job and received a substantial payment for her troubles. She returned to bless her family with some of her unexpected wealth and found Dirk in the garden on a school day.

She was livid! She called his mother. "Come and get your child, Heather. Mom and Dad have turned him into a day laborer without pay."

When his mother came for him two weeks later, he was nine years old. He remembered the occasion vividly. He had been at the front of the cramped cottage where his grandparents had their home, sitting on the steps while his aunt and a contractor she had hired discussed building over the old house. They discussed square footage and the logistics of expanding the small, dilapidated structure into something more spacious and modern. His aunt had many ideas, while the contractor scribbled notes and occasionally asked questions.

"I want a 16 by 16 feet bedroom," his aunt said.

"That's 256 square feet," Dirk said.

Both the contractor and his aunt looked over at him.

"Where did you learn that?" his aunt asked.

"I saw Micky's math workbook," Dirk responded. "It's really fun."

Micky was his cousin, who usually played with him when he got in from school.

"He thinks math is fun, and they have him milking cows and running wild without shoes," Verona breathed. "We have a future genius sitting here on the steps when they should have nurtured his curiosity. This family is cursed with ignorance and a lack of sense."

"Don't say that," the contractor said. "You got out."

"Only because I didn't live with my parents," Verona replied. "Mrs. Green, a retired teacher, took an interest in me. She was a widow who lived alone and wanted a well-behaved young girl to stay with her. She admired me at school; she said I was polite and neat. Back in those days, my parents had to send us to school. Our politician at the time, the first woman politician in this district, had someone going around and taking note of school-aged children who weren't attending school. Every summer, we got our uniforms, shoes, and bags. The parents had no excuse not to send us.

"Back then, this district was highly illiterate. The politician, who was also a former educator, found that alarming. Anyway, illiteracy aside, my parents had no ambition for us. You know some people who would want better for their children? My parents lacked that zeal. If Mrs. Green had not taken me, I would be like Tracy and Terrence, doing subsistence farming and barely having two cents to rub together."

"What about his mother?" the contractor asked, pointing to Dirk.

"Heather, the youngest. She was so pretty, Daddy didn't want to send her to the shop alone. One of us had to accompany her," Verona laughed. "She could have modeled and used her looks as a stepping stone to greater things, like work on television or hosting programs. So many other girls do it. But alas, out here in this backwater, there was no opportunity.

"And my parents didn't have that ambition for us, as I said. I had left the area by then, and I didn't want Heather to end up like my other siblings after she graduated high school. So I got a job for her. A friend of a friend of mine knew of an opening as a housekeeper at a villa in High Gate.

"The plan was for her to do skills training at the vocational school in town and stay there," Verona sighed. "It was a sweet deal. The people who owned the place, the James', were rich. They were from around these parts and migrated years before. They just wanted a trustworthy person to keep their place livable until they or their children stopped by, usually in the summer.."

"I know of them," the contractor nodded. "Simon James is a big deal in New York. They're from the same district as my mother."

"Yes, that's them," Verona nodded. Six months after my sister started working for them, their son Lancelot came by to stay. He was a fine art painter and pretty good, too—his work is in galleries. He wanted a peaceful and quiet place to paint, so he returned to his parents' country.

"And wouldn't you know it, he took one look at my sister, and they fell in love. They had a thing for months, and then she got pregnant. He promised to marry her, but he met with a bike accident and died before he could. The James's allowed Heather to live at their place while she was pregnant. Lance was their only son, and they were excited to have a grandchild from him.

"But then, my sister had spurned a guy, Mario, one of Lancelot's friends, a few months before. And wouldn't you know it, he told the Jame's that the child was his and that my sister was a liar.

"They kicked her out, heavily pregnant, so she had to come back here to live with our parents in this broken-down house. I had to take care of her and the baby while she got back on her feet. She worked in town at a bar to make ends meet, and then she got the opportunity to be a nanny in Cayman.

"The plan was to send for Lance when she was settled. But there never was a right time. I warned her to take him away from this place. I thought our parents would revert to type, and just as I thought, they did.

"Luckily, though, Heather married a rich man and moved back to Jamaica a month ago. She said she would come by for Lance when they settled on a house in Kingston. They are actively house hunting, but right now, it is chaotic. They live in a one-bedroom while they look around. So, any time now, my nephew will be rescued, as it should be. If she hadn't had those arrangements, I would take him myself."

Dirk's ears had perked up. He had listened to the story quietly. He had not heard any of that before. He lay down and looked up at the sky. The air was thick with the scent of freshly turned soil and the hum of summer insects.

He remembered feeling a mix of confusion and hope—confusion because he couldn't understand why his mother didn't come for him now, but he was hopeful because the prospect of his mother rescuing him from his life of drudgery was too much for his little heart to bear.

He barely heard his aunt describe her vision to expand her parents' house, speaking of a larger kitchen and extra bedrooms. His mind wandered to the possibilities of leaving his grandparents' house, where he would be free from the chores that had become his daily burden and get to see his mom again. He had not seen her in four years. Talking on the phone had not been enough. He didn't remember her much.

As if he had conjured her up out of his mind, a shiny car stopped at the gate, and a sophisticated woman who looked like one of those actresses on television stepped out of the vehicle. She wore a fitted dress and curly hair that hit her in the small of her back. She was with a tall guy who wouldn't release her hand.

"Speak of the devil!" Verona exclaimed. "Heather! I was just talking about you!"

Heather hugged her sister tightly and then turned to him. "Oh, my baby, my baby. I am so sorry. I will never leave you again."

After she had cried and slobbered all over him, she cupped his face and said, "I am taking you to Kingston with me. I will never return you to this sad little place again."

"Don't say that," Verona said. "I will overhaul this place and build a guest suite just for you."

His grandparents had come to the front after they heard the car drive up, and there had been a shouting match between his mother and his grandparents. The words "cruel" and "child abuse" came up often. While Heather was busy fuming, the man she had come with stooped to his level and looked him in the eye.

"My name is Garrick Morgan. I am your mother's husband."

They shook hands.

"What's your name?"

"Dirk Lance Cauldwell," Dirk stammered, "but I prefer the name Lance."

"I promise you this, Lance," Garrick said, "I will take good care of you and your mother. I am so sorry your life has been so rough until now."

They took him to Kingston. His mother bundled him into the car without even taking a bag.

"They had him clothed in rags and working around the clock," she sobbed. "I can't believe my parents took all the money I sent for his upkeep and bought livestock and then turned around and treated him like a slave."

Dirk sat in the backseat of the car, his heart pounding with relief and fear. As they drove away from the only home he had known, he felt a strange sense of liberation. The rolling hills and fields receded into the distance, replaced by the bustling cityscape of Kingston. It was overwhelming but exhilarating.

For the first time, he felt that his life could be different. He held tightly to the promise of a new beginning, determined to make the most of this second chance.

"Don't worry, honey, it will be all right," Garrick muttered intermittently while his mother ranted and raved about how they had treated him.

"They haven't sent him to school since I left," she whispered. "Verona said she thought I knew. How could I have known? I sent money for his school supplies every summer and every month. I sent his lunch money and extras. What on earth did they do with that money? I'll tell you what they did, they bought cows and pigs. I can't believe my parents were so mercenary. My mother told me with her own mouth that he was doing well in school."

It was his first time out of the district. He vaguely heard the rest of his mother's gripes with her parents. He did hear, though, that she would enroll him in school as soon as possible.

He found out much later that his stepfather, Garrick, was quite wealthy. Garrick owned an insurance firm. He had literally bumped into Heather in Cayman and instantly knew she was going to be special to him. Two months later, they married. Garrick treated him like a much-loved son, and his life improved.

It wasn't long after going to school that he and his teachers discovered that he was a genius with figures. By the third form, he was doing advanced mathematics, and soon, he was winning math competitions left and right. Garrick encouraged him every step of the way, providing him with resources and opportunities he never would have dreamed of before. He did a double first degree in actuarial science and forensic accounting at the University of the West Indies and a master's in statistics and economics.

Through the years, he remained close to his aunt, Verona. She valued his opinion highly, so it was no surprise when she called him to give an opinion on a villa she had recently bought in Highgate.

It was in the same area where James had their villa and where his mother met his father. It was a beautiful neighborhood, with the sea in the distance and houses nestled among lush, green hills. The air was crisp and clean, carrying the faint scent of saltwater and blooming flowers.

His aunt's villa was a stunning, white-washed structure with large windows that let in abundant natural light. It stood on a gently sloping hill, offering a panoramic view of the sea and the surrounding landscape.

They were walking along the road in the neighborhood. Verona's excitement was palpable. "Let me tell you, Lance," she said, "while growing up, I never thought I'd own a place like this. I'd always see these places with spacious verandas, gardens filled with exotic plants, and infinity pools that seemed to merge seamlessly with the horizon. And I would say, 'One day, one day, Verona!' This is the day, nephew. The house even has its own private jetty! We are definitely going to need a boat. No, not an ordinary boat, a yacht!"

Dirk chuckled.

"I've worked hard for this and wanted to share it with you first. It's our little piece of paradise," she smiled, her face lighting up with pride. "You are my designated heir. So, in effect, this place is just as much mine as yours. I have already put your name on the title. This will be our first business venture together, our just-in-case income. Maybe we can buy more places when you start making your own money. We need to create an LLC and make things official. But in the meantime, this is the flagship villa. What should we call it?"

"Sea Glass," Dirk laughed. "The sea looks like glass from here."

"Sea Glass Villa," Verona laughed heartily. "I like it!"

A vehicle passed them as they were grinning together, slowed down, and turned back. In the car was an older couple, a very fair woman and her darker husband.

"Lance!" the lady said, "Oh my God!"

"Hello," Dirk looked at both of them curiously. He had never seen them before.

"It's not Lance," the man said. "He is too young to be Lance."

"I am actually called Lance," Dirk said, "it is my middle name, actually. I am Dirk Lance Cauldwell."

"Oh my," the woman whispered, "your mother is Heather Cauldwell?"

Dirk nodded.

"What have we done?" the man said, his voice heavy. "We are your grandparents, Simon and Margaret Cauldwell."

"Wait a minute," Verona said for the first time. "You people abandoned my sister when she was pregnant and could have used your help."

"We are so sorry," tears were in Margaret's eyes. "It's just that Mario convinced us that he was the father and not our son. He told us to back off. We were so devastated, we asked Heather to leave."

"That guy Mario has much to answer for," Verona huffed. "Heather had a tough time after leaving your employ; she went home to our parent's house with nothing."

"Well, Mario is dead," Simon said, "he died two years after our Lance did."

"How?" Verona frowned.

"Suicide," Simon said heavily, "he had a lot of things to deal with, apparently. We have always wondered what happened to the child, well, you."

Dirk smiled. "Well, now you know."

Simon looked at Dirk. "Well, now that we found you, we can't lose touch."

Chapter Four

Dirk rose from his seat and made his way to the patio. His life had unfolded in a series of intriguing coincidences. For instance, Sea Glass Villa, the villa Alex had rented for the weekend, was partially his. He co-owned six others with his aunt across the island. They were all managed by a management company.

Another twist of fate was discovering that his grandfather, Simon, owned a Forensic Accounting Firm in New York. It seemed his affinity for numbers ran in the family; Simon was also a genius in the field and was thrilled to learn about Dirk's focus on mathematics, finance, and accounting. His aunt Pamella was the managing director.

After completing his master's, Dirk pondered various career paths, with forensic accounting not initially ranking high on his list. However, the field proved captivating, drawing him to it.

Simon was eager for Dirk to adopt the James surname and

immediately join his firm in New York. Dirk deliberated extensively over the phone with his aunt about the decision.

"Go for it," Verona advised. "You are rightfully a James. Your father was a US citizen, so you won't encounter many obstacles in claiming citizenship. The salary sounds good, plus, it's your grandfather's firm. I don't see a problem."

Dirk hesitated. "I've developed feelings for someone. I wanted to stick around and see if something could develop. I've put things on hold until I finish my degree and she graduates high school."

"There will always be someone," Verona remarked. "You're only twenty-one. You can't trust your feelings at that age. How old is she?"

"Eighteen."

"She can't trust her feelings either," Verona snorted. "As a teenage girl, I was notorious for being unpredictable and impulsive. Emotions run high at that age, and what seems like a perfect match today might not feel the same tomorrow. Trust me on this. I know what I'm talking about—I've had two failed marriages."

Dirk sighed, grappling with his aunt's words while wrestling with his emotions. "I know, but it feels different with her. She's special and I don't want to lose that chance."

"I understand, Dirk. But you also have to think about your future. This opportunity with your grandfather's firm is a once-in-a-lifetime chance. It could set you up for life. Relationships can be nurtured from a distance too, especially in this day and age with all the technology we have."

"It wouldn't be fair to burden her with a long-distance relationship. I don't even know if she's as serious about me as I am about her. I've tried hard to keep some distance between us when I only want to draw her closer."

"Don't push it," Verona said, "if it's meant to be, you will find each other again."

"I suppose you're right. It's hard to let go of something that feels so important."

"Trust me, I've been there," Verona said. "And I can tell you from experience that life has a way of working out, often in ways we least expect. Focus on building a solid foundation for your future, and the rest will follow."

He had taken the job and changed his surname. A name change was relatively easy, including updating his school documents. The red carpet was rolled out upon his arrival in New York City, where most of the James family lived—his grandparents, two aunts, their husbands, and children. His grandparents resided on the Upper East Side, which has a view of Central Park.

During their first dinner, Dirk listened intently as his grandparents and aunts recounted stories of his father, Lancelot James. He was a free-spirited artist who had captured the hearts of many with his creativity. They spoke of his adventurous spirit, love for travel, and passion for life. And they showed Dirk the breathtaking paintings he had created.

"It's painful to call you Lance," his aunt Pamella had said. "You look so much like him…can I call you Dirk instead?"

"Sure," Dirk nodded.

And so he got used to being called Dirk or DL. He was fine with it. Even his mother and stepfather had adjusted to calling him Dirk. It was only his family in the hills that still called him Lance. He took it all in stride.

Two months ago, his stepfather had called him for help.

"I have some shares in a wealth management company called LAD. They are going through auditing at the moment. The auditor is someone I know pretty well; I saw him at dinner last night, and he said he was uncomfortable with the books."

"Uncomfortable?" Dirk had asked sleepily. "That's vague."

"It is, but he said he can't quite put his finger on what is going on. He thinks there are discrepancies in their financial records, but he needs help to figure it out. Whatever it is, it is making one of the best auditors in the business uncomfortable. Could you take a look at it, Dirk? You're good with numbers; you'll figure it out."

Dirk's mind immediately snapped to attention. Despite his exhaustion, the mention of financial discrepancies piqued his interest. Besides, he would do anything for Garrick.

"What does looking at it mean?" Dirk asked. "Do you want to send me all the relevant documents, and I'll see what I can find?"

"No," Garrick said, "I want you out here, working undercover. I think this needs a deep investigation. That's what Paulo said. He was the one who mentioned you. He read the article about you in Diaspora Magazine, where they described you as a Sherlock Holmes-type young genius who can sniff out fraud in your sleep. And how the whole financial world is in awe of you. He knows we are family, so he told me to ask you for help."

Dirk chuckled. "That article in Diaspora Magazine is the gift that keeps on giving. The journalist, Milly Monroe, hyped me up a bit too much."

"Ah, but it was true," Garrick chuckled. "You solved all the cases she mentioned. Your mother bought a stack of the magazines and handed them to her friends. She reads various parts of the interview out loud before the kids get ready for school. My favorite quote is: 'The handsome, urbane financier Dirk James is a numbers genius; he is one of a new wave of young black professional men who are redefining success in the financial world. With his sharp intellect and innovative approach, Dirk not only solves complex financial puzzles but also inspires others to follow in his footsteps. His work is not just about numbers; it's about creating lasting change and opening doors for future generations.'"

Dirk chuckled. "She has read it so many times. I know it by heart."

"I always knew you were a genius," Garrick said. "I am not surprised that others are finding that out."

"Ah, Dad," Dirk smiled, "I am who I am and where I am mainly because of you and Mom. How is she?"

"Good. Great. She is heading out to the gym now."

"Hi, Baby," his mother said, close to the phone.

"Hi, Mom."

"I'll call you later," Heather said. Check the family group. I posted a video of Emily winning a silver medal in her ballet competition yesterday. In a few months, she will compete in the regional competition."

"Okay," Dirk responded. At seven years old, his youngest sister was shaping up to be quite a ballet dancer.

"Back to the topic at hand," Garrick said when his mother left. "Didn't you say you work from home sometimes?"

"I do," Dirk said.

"So, can you work from home here in Jamaica for a while? We miss you, you know. You haven't been out here since last summer."

"I was busy with that case that earned me the glowing article in Diaspora Magazine."

"I know," Garrick said.

Dirk looked out at the New York skyline. It was snowing. He had long gotten past the wide-eyed wonder of seeing snow. He remembered how excited he had been to see it for the first time. However, after six years of living in New York, it had become more of an inconvenience than a novelty.

He longed for blue skies, natural heat, and crisp air. He also missed his mother's cooking and the noise and mayhem that his four siblings, aged five to fifteen, brought with them. He would arrange things with Pamella, his aunt, and his immediate boss. He still needed to wrap up a few cases but didn't foresee a problem returning home.

He would use the pool house as his base; it was far enough away from the main house to get some quiet time to work and just a short walk to be a part of the family life when he needed company.

"Okay, I'll do it."

And that was why he was back here.

Following the clues to solve the case that had led him right back to Cayenne Aubry. He would have to avoid Cayenne to maintain his cover. The one girl who his mind kept drifting back to over the years.

Seeing her today had been like a jolt to his system. She looked even more stunning than he remembered, with a grace and confidence that made his heart ache with nostalgia.

He remembered when they were neighbors; he had anticipated a knock every day at four when she came home from school. He had called them their chat sessions. She had been such a breath of fresh air. He had tried resisting liking her, but it hadn't worked. The more they talked, the more he anticipated seeing her. By the tenth month of staying next door, he had reluctantly grown attached to Cayenne.

Cayenne dutifully reported to him her extracurricular activities, thoughts about boys, career aspirations, and future plans.

Her future plans coincided with his future plans. He eagerly listened to what she had to say. Despite what his aunt thought, he wanted to explore something with Cayenne. Maybe they could get serious over the summer.

"I don't want to go to college yet," Cayenne said. "Cinnamon thinks I should, but my mom supports my plans. She said she would help me every step of the way. I am going to take her up on her offer."

"What are the plans again?" Dirk asked, eager to hear.

"I am going to cosmetology school after graduation, which is six months, and then I will get my license and open my own shop. I even know the location already. It's beside my mom's wig store," Cayenne explained.

Dirk nodded. "You are quite sure what you want to do," he mused, "most people your age don't have a clue. I still wonder what I will do after this, and I am four years older than you. What was the process like, deciding?"

"Easy," Cayenne shrugged. "I like to do hair. I love to see people looking good. I spend hours watching transformation videos. I want to be the one helping people feel better about themselves.

"I will do a professional makeup artistry course this summer in California, and then I will be a girl Friday on a movie set. My mother's current boyfriend hooked me up. He is an actor. I have to move fast before they break up; I do not see this relationship lasting long."

Dirk nodded.

"What are you going to do?" Cayenne looked at him, her hazel eyes inquisitive. He had given her sparse details about himself. But today, he felt like opening up a little.

"I will hand in my final project next week. And then I think I am going to migrate."

"No, Lance!" Cayenne widened her eyes exaggeratedly. "But we haven't even kissed yet! Plus, we need to plan our wedding."

Dirk laughed. He couldn't help it.

Cayenne laughed with him. "I was only half serious."

"I know," Dirk said. "But we have our whole lives ahead of us."

"You don't know that for certain," Cayenne sighed. "I may never see you again."

"I think we will see each other again," Dirk said. "When the time is right."

That had been their last conversation. He had always regretted leaving without telling her a proper goodbye.

Six years later, the time was still not convenient.

He should have prepared himself for this eventuality, that someone would recognize him from the past or even from that article in Diaspora Magazine. When no one from the office pointed him out, he had begun to get comfortable. Usually, when people knew his role in their organization, they treated him weirdly, especially the guilty ones.

He couldn't tell Cayenne what he was up to now; Alex was her friend. They were quite close, so she would blow his cover. He would have to keep up the pretense that he didn't know her, at least for this weekend.

He was making the right choice by keeping Cayenne temporarily in the dark. He inhaled deeply and looked at the night view. Usually, night sea views were boring, but this one was different. The moonlight danced on the waves, creating a shimmering path across the water. The distant lights from the harbor added a soft, golden glow to the scene, making it almost magical. It was a nice house; of all their properties, Aunt Verona visited this one the most. He loved Sea Glass Villas.

He saw movement to his right. It was Cayenne; she was clutching a pillow and sheet. He moved closer to the dark, waiting to see her next move.

Chapter Five

Cayenne tossed and turned, kicked off the sheets and put the pillow over her head. Sanya preferred warmer temperatures for falling asleep, but she was partial to feeling as chilly as possible. She had okayed raising the temperature setting on the AC, but now she couldn't sleep.

She resentfully listened to Sanya snoring away while she suffered in the room's warmth.

Coupled with that were thoughts of Alex and Dirk.

She resented that Alex had thrown her out of her previous room, where she would have been alone with her AC at whatever temperature she wished.

If she had her own room, she would be fast asleep by now, or would she be thinking about Dirk?

She couldn't stop thinking about the guy. It was obvious that he had avoided her at dinner. Maybe she had made him uncomfortable when she had talked to him about Lance. Or maybe he was genuinely into Alex. He talked to her a lot.

They had even disappeared onto the patio and walked by the beach in the moonlight.

Maybe they were together right now.

A shaft of jealousy hit her. The truth was that Dirk James looked too much like Lance for her to be neutral about him and Alex being together.

That's it. She wouldn't lie in bed and belabor the whole scenario in her mind. She was going to get up and go on the patio. The lounge chairs seemed as if they would be comfy, and the air outside would be chillier at this time of the morning than what she was experiencing.

Maybe she would listen to a podcast; there was one about sheep farming that didn't fail to lull her to sleep. She tiptoed and opened the patio doors wider.

Sanya didn't shift, judging by her deep, consistent snores. She grabbed a sheet and a pillow and headed to the lounge chair furthest from the door which would take her closer to Dirk's side of the patio.

He probably wasn't in his room. He was probably with Alex.

She sighed. Who Alex spent time with was none of her business. Her friend was young and in love and knew about the pitfalls of falling into bed with someone before knowing them or being in a committed relationship. Alex had done it so many times before, gotten heartbroken, or lost interest in the flavor of the month that she could write a book about it.

Surprisingly, Alex was more sexually liberal.

Though she was the church girl from the nuclear family, stable parents, and matching pajamas at Christmas time. Alex even gave lectures to her church youth group about purity culture and waiting till marriage. The hypocrisy of it all had always boggled Cayenne's mind.

Cayenne had not grown up religious though her nanny,

Trudy, used to take them to church when she was between four and seven. She could vaguely remember the loud music and the dancing. It was one of those charismatic churches where people spoke in tongues and didn't leave until the spirit had left the building.

But then the pastor had been caught in a sex scandal with an underage girl, and Anise had freaked out. Her mother had literally blown her top.

"Don't take them there again!" She remembered Anise yelling. "Never!"

"But predators are everywhere, madam," Trudy had protested. "There are other good people there."

"If you take them again. You are fired!" Anise yelled. Her mother had zero tolerance for child molesters.

That had been her only brush with church and religion until she started going with Alex to youth group meetings on Thursday nights. She usually enjoyed their presentations, but she always found it ironic that though Alex was the churchgoer, she was her voice of reason and moral compass.

Her unconventional background should have indicated otherwise. Her mother was the notorious Anise Cooper, whose revolving door of partners was legendary, and her father was the infamous Paul Aubry, who was currently serving time in prison for child molestation.

Anise had caught him touching her inappropriately when she was just three years old. Anise almost killed him.

That was apparently not the first time he had tried it with both Cayenne and Sage.

Cayenne didn't remember any of it; she didn't remember her father, how he looked, his voice, nothing, but she had grown up quite aware that she had been a sex abuse victim and that her father was in prison because of that very reason. It had made her extremely cautious about trusting men.

That caution had disappeared when she had met Lance Cauldwell. She had been so deep in her little teenage crush that she would have done anything to be with him.

Luckily, Lance had not taken her seriously or where would she be now? Heartbroken, that's what.

When she had just met him and was a little overeager with her hero worship, Lance had told her frankly, "I like you, Cayenne, but you are going through a crush. This is a phase you are experiencing. You will snap out of it, find someone else, and pay me dust by next week."

She had never snapped out of it. Cayenne closed her eyes. Instead of listening to her podcast, she thought about Lance.

She drew the next lounge chair closer and put her iPad and headphones on it. Outside was cooler than her room; it was downright nippy. She pulled the sheet tighter and snuggled into her pillow. Hopefully, it won't rain tonight.

Was that movement she saw over on Dirk James' side of the patio? No, it was probably the breeze. Each patio was semi-private, divided by low walls. If one was limber enough, they could climb the low wall dividing the areas and check to see what was happening.

She would not be caught climbing that wall.

Besides, she was feeling a little bit sleepy. She snuggled into her makeshift bed and inhaled her fragrant pillow. She would think about Lance until she fell asleep. She hadn't done that in years.

Chapter Six

Sometime in the Past

"Where's our food?" Cayenne's belly rumbled.

"We did order a lot," Sage chuckled. "We should never order food when we are hungry." Sage opened the window and peeped out, then gasped.

"The delivery guy is here?" Cayenne asked.

"Nope, it's a guy though. You have to see him. He is moving in next door."

"I'm not interested," Cayenne murmured. "I have exams tomorrow and am too hungry to appreciate anybody right now."

"Oh, child," Sage said. "If you see this guy, exams will be the last thing on your mind. Food will be at the bottom of your list."

Cayenne hooted with laughter. "He can't be that great. Describe him."

"He's about six feet tall. Probably 6'1," Sage said. "He's brown, about the same shade as my heavenly honey foundation, and built like a runner."

"Long-distance or sprints?" Cayenne asked lazily.

"Sprints," Sage said. "Oh, my. You should see his muscles flex as he removes his bags from the car."

"What's he wearing?" Cayenne closed her economics textbook; she hadn't been concentrating on it anyway.

"Blue jeans. They fit perfectly. He has a slight bow in his leg. Ooh la la."

Cayenne laughed. "So, just blue jeans? He's shirtless?"

"Nope, he's wearing a white T-shirt with writing on it," Sage answered promptly.

"What does it say?" Cayenne asked. "You can tell a man by the writing on his T-shirt."

"Really?" Sage rolled her eyes. "Where'd you hear that?"

"It's common sense. If a person, male or female, has a message on their shirt, you assume things about them. I'd assume they would be playful or humorous if they had something on it, like a 'warning, this is not a drill' with a picture of a hammer. That one always cracks me up."

Sage chuckled. "Yep. And if they have one that says, 'I am weird, stay away,' I would stay away."

"That's not what your fantasy neighbor guy has on his, is it?" Cayenne asked.

"Nope," Sage grinned. "His T-shirt says, 'Live well, laugh often, love much.' Isn't that sweet and positive?"

Cayenne smiled. "It is. I am intrigued. I am almost moved to get up and see what you are seeing. But I know you are pulling my leg."

"I am not," Sage whispered. "He really is fine."

"Describe his eyes," Cayenne said lazily.

"I can't see them," Sage said. "He looks like he is

unpacking quite a bit of stuff. He's probably going to be here for a while."

She always played the people-watching game with Sage. Her sister would sit in the chair closest to the window and report on all the happenings in their small townhouse complex. There were just eight houses, but it was a constant source of entertainment for them; the houses on both their left and right were short-term rentals. Last month, they lived beside a couple who had just won the lottery. The month before that was a married athlete who was having an affair with a well-known minister of the gospel.

When he came over, Cayenne would join Sage at the window, and they would covertly watch the comings and goings.

Their sister Cinnamon was technically their guardian, and it was her place that they lived. She would listen in wide-eyed astonishment as they detailed how interesting their little neighborhood could get. Cinnamon was always working and not privy to the drama like they were.

"Oh my," Sage whispered furiously, "he looked my way."

"So his eyes are…" Cayenne prompted.

"Medium brown. The color of warm chocolate," Sage whispered back. "And they're framed by the longest lashes I've ever seen on a guy."

Cayenne chuckled. "Now you're just exaggerating."

"I swear I'm not!" Sage insisted. "You'll have to see for yourself."

Cayenne sighed; she didn't want to waste any energy and be disappointed. "Well, if he's that distracting, I might have to take a peek."

"Trust me, it'll be worth it," Sage said with a grin. "He is a beautiful man."

"Good for him," Cayenne snickered. "But I don't believe

you."

"You'd better come and see him before he goes inside."

Cayenne sighed and got up. "If you make me waste my time on some ugly guy, it won't be pretty. I'll make you pay for this, Missy."

She opened the curtain wider, looked outside, and gasped. "Good Lord, he's fine. Why didn't you say something?"

"I have been saying something," Sage said. "What do you think my running commentary was about?"

"But this type of gorgeousness does not occur every day," Cayenne said a bit too loudly.

He stopped unpacking, looked across at the window, and grinned.

"Even white teeth," Sage whispered. "I bet he got braces in the past. I hope that's my final result after I take mine out. We have something in common. I am going to strike up a conversation with him about it."

Cayenne was speechless. They watched silently as he carried his things inside. And then a pocketbook fell from his things, and they waited to see if he would notice.

"So which of us will tell him that his pocketbook fell?" Sage asked dramatically.

"I'll do it," Cayenne said. "It is my sworn duty as the oldest to help our neighbor."

Sage laughed. "Cinnamon is the oldest. We should wait until she comes home."

"Oh, shut it. He's mine," Cayenne said. She looked in the mirror in the hallway. "How do I look?"

"Awful," Sage said. "I've seen you look better."

Cayenne laughed. "I don't care. I am going in."

She was in her boy shorts and tank top, and her hair was in a casual top knot, piled high with curly tendrils sticking out all over. It could use a good brushing. If it were slicked back and looked polished, she would make a better impression, but she was loathed to go upstairs and miss her opportunity to meet the guy next door.

Besides, her face was glowing, and she looked healthy. She always got compliments on her looks, whether she wore makeup or not. She had inherited her father's honey-gold skin, green hazel eyes, and her mother's cheekbones and height. She couldn't tell how many times she had been asked to model. It wasn't just her; Cinnamon and Sage, too, especially Cinnamon, who was the carbon copy of their modelesque mother.

But Anise always vetoed whatever offers they got. "Model your inner beauty," Anise would say. "In the end, that's all that matters. Work on exercising your kindness, be a light to your fellow man, and make people admire you for your goodness, not your looks."

She didn't know why that little gem was playing in her head as she sauntered outside with Sage giggling behind the curtain.

She bent down slowly and exaggeratedly and picked up the pocketbook when he came out of the house.

"Wow," he grinned as he looked at her legs.

She straightened up, arching her back like a dancer, and smiled. "My sister and I watched you move in, and I saw this fall."

"Yes, I just saw it," he smiled. "I was heading out to have something to eat. My name is Lance Cauldwell, and yours?"

"Cayenne Cauldwell."

He raised his eyebrows.

"I mean, Cayenne Aubry," she laughed.

"Lovely to meet you, Miss Aubry," he nodded, "and thank you for my pocketbook."

She handed it to him. "You don't have to go out to eat.

Come and join us; we just ordered takeout. My sister was looking out for the delivery guy, so she was by the window. Otherwise, we mind our own business about sixty percent of the time."

Lance grinned. "So it wasn't to spy on me?"

"Not entirely," Cayenne said. "We are hungry too. Usually, one of us would cook, but it's our takeout day. We get one day a week to do it according to the household budget. The government is quite strict on that."

"Oh," Lance smiled. "Who is the minister of finance?"

"My sister, Cinnamon. She is also the head of government over here in Spice Land."

"Your sister's name is really Cinnamon?"

"Yup," Cayenne nodded. "My mother's name is Anise, and my grandmother's is Rosemary."

"And the one watching me through the window?" Lance asked.

"Sage," Cayenne grinned.

"My goodness," Lance grinned. "It's really Spice Land."

"My family is fairly interesting," Cayenne said. "If you come over now, we'll tell you more. Don't worry about robbing us of the food. We generally order too much anyway."

"Are you sure that wouldn't be too much of a bother?" Lance asked.

"No bother at all," Cayenne said. "It's the least we can do. It's a neighborly gesture; welcome to the neighborhood. We are nice people, except for Mrs. Linton in House 3; she gets grumpy if you pet her dog."

Lance chuckled. "Okay, note to self: do not pet Mrs. Linton's dog."

"And her daughter Kelsey, she's a model; you may have seen her in several advertisements. She may be pretty, but she is intellectually challenged. So keep away."

"It's true, Kelsey is dumb as a doorknob," Sage said when Lance entered the townhouse. "The delivery guy is here."

She jumped up. "Right on time!"

They laid the food on the table and invited Lance to sit down.

It was a large spread from their favorite Italian restaurant, Bud and Sally's. Sage had ordered various dishes, from cheesy lasagna to creamy fettuccine Alfredo, accompanied by garlic breadsticks and fresh salads.

"Wow," Lance said when he sat, "you were right. This is a lot of food."

"So what do you do, Lance?" Sage was the first to ask.

"Currently, I am a student," Lance said. "I am doing my master's in statistics and economics. I am also house-sitting for Mr. Henry, who owns the apartment next door. He is my father's friend and doesn't want another renter. He may keep or sell it; I am just staying there while he decides."

"Oh yes," Cayenne nodded. "The last tenants, the lottery winners, were rowdy. They argued and fought every day. I am surprised the building is still standing. The police seemed to be here every day after they moved in."

Lance nodded.

"Before that, was the drug dealer," Sage grinned. "His friends looked suspicious. Reminds me of a boyfriend mom had."

"Your mother? Anise?" Lance asked.

"She's famous," Sage volunteered. "She is currently in the papers for dating Croy Landers, the basketball player."

Cayenne kicked her under the table. She didn't want to discuss their mother and her checkered love life.

"Why'd you kick me for?" Sage pouted. "Mom is famous."

"For the wrong things," Cayenne groaned. "We don't lead

a conversation with what she is doing."

Lance chuckled. "I pay attention mostly to the finance sections of the paper."

"Good," Cayenne said feelingly.

"But I know about Anise Cooper," Lance said. "You would have to be living out in the woods with no communication with the real world not to have heard of her. Besides, wasn't she just telling her life story in an interview?"

Cayenne sighed. And here it would come. He would assume they were tainted somehow. If only Anise had not done that interview. It had been filled with too much information, including the Paul Aubry time in her life when she proudly told the world she almost killed her ex-husband because he was molesting their children.

Cayenne knew the moment Lance put two and two together. He looked between the two of them and widened his eyes. "You are the girls who were…"

"Yes, we are," Cayenne sighed. "I don't want to talk about it."

"But that means you are just children," he began to look uncomfortable, "if this happened fourteen years ago…I thought you were older!"

"Thank you," Sage smiled. "I have been told that I look eighteen."

"Nobody tells you that," Cayenne snorted. She looked at him. "I'll be eighteen in six months, and you are invited to my birthday party. I am planning it from now. My mom said I should go big."

"When you said you were studying, I thought college, not high school," Lance said in horror. "I actually thought about dating you."

"Really!" Cayenne squealed.

"I can't date you now. You are a high schooler, and I

am doing my master's. Besides, your mother said in her interview that she will happily shoot any man that messes with her precious children."

Cayenne grinned; there was genuine fear in his eyes. "Mess as in trouble, harm, play a fast one. You don't want to do that, do you?"

"No," Lance shook his head. "No, of course not."

"Then we are fine. Anise doesn't live here. I told you Cinnamon is the head of government here, and as far as I know, she is not as trigger-happy as Anise."

Lance sighed and shook his head. "I instantly liked you, Cayenne, but it won't work."

"Wait," Cayenne said, "we can be friends, right?"

"I don't know," Lance said.

Chapter Seven

Cayenne opened her eyes when she heard footsteps approaching. She sat up abruptly, peering into the dark, her heart beating rapidly. She had been so caught up in her reminiscence she hadn't heard anyone coming.

"Don't be frightened, it's just me, Dirk," came a familiar voice.

"Oh," Cayenne inhaled raggedly. "What are you doing up?"

"I was standing on the patio when you came out here and started spreading your bed in the lounge chair," he whispered. I watched you for a while. I didn't want to disturb you, but I heard a chuckle and realized you weren't asleep."

"I wasn't chuckling," Cayenne murmured.

"You made a laughing sound," Dirk said, lying in the lounge chair beside her. "I could hear you from my section of the patio. I thought you had seen me and were signaling you were awake and ready to talk."

"What time is it?" Cayenne asked wearily.

"Twelve forty-one," Dirk said.

"I thought you were avoiding me," Cayenne said. "I wanted to apologize for how I greeted you today."

"No need to apologize," Dirk said, sinking in the lounge chair beside her. "I was avoiding you."

"Why?" Cayenne asked.

"I didn't want to remind you too much of your crush, Lance Cauldwell," Dirk said. "I thought I would give you some space to come to terms with the idea that I am not him."

Cayenne grunted, "Too late."

"It's actually nicer out here," Dirk said after a brief silence. "Maybe I should go and get my pillow and sheet."

Cayenne laughed. "I am not out here because of the novelty of it. I am out here because of Sanya; she cannot sleep with the AC, and I got too warm. Out here seemed like a better plan."

"Ah," Dirk said.

"Alex kicked me out of the room when you showed up," Cayenne said grumpily.

"You can sleep in the room if you want," Dirk said. "I like it out here."

"No," Cayenne looked at him in the half-light. "I am already comfortable. I was going to listen to a podcast and then fall asleep. But I started thinking about…"

"Lance," Dirk turned to her. "You know you are not the only one who has had a case of limerence; I had one, too, when I was in high school."

"Limerence?" Cayenne whistled. "I haven't heard that word in a while. What's the difference between limerence and a crush or even love? How did you know what you had and then tell me about your high school limerence?"

Dirk chuckled. "Okay, let me preface this answer by saying I am a numbers man; I just know the basics regarding things like love, limerence, and crushes. But I'll make an attempt to sound knowledgeable."

Cayenne laughed. "Now, this I have to hear."

"Limerence is kind of like a crush on steroids," Dirk began, leaning back and looking up at the stars. "It's this intense, almost obsessive infatuation with someone. You can't get them out of your head, you overanalyze every interaction, and you feel this overwhelming need to have your feelings reciprocated."

"Sounds familiar," Cayenne murmured.

"A crush," Dirk continued, "is more casual. It's admiration mixed with attraction. You might daydream about the person, but it's not all-consuming. And love—well, love is deeper. It's about knowing someone inside and out, accepting their flaws, and building something lasting together."

Cayenne nodded, her interest piqued. "So how did you know you had limerence in high school?"

Dirk sighed, a nostalgic smile playing on his lips. "My English teacher, Miss Rebecca Lewis. She was smart, funny, beautiful, and wore the tightest skirts to class. I couldn't focus on anything else when she was around. I'd analyze every word she said and replay our conversations in my head a million times. It reached the point where I couldn't sleep or eat. My English grades started slipping. I was a mess."

"What happened with Rebecca?" Cayenne laughed softly.

"Eventually, I told her how I felt," Dirk said, his tone a bit somber. "She was kind about it; she let me down gently and told me she didn't feel the same way, and even if she did, a relationship between us would be inappropriate blah blah. It crushed me then, but looking back, it was a blessing. Telling her forced me to confront my feelings and realize that I was in love with the idea of her, not the real person."

Cayenne was silent for a moment, absorbing his words. "Your situation is totally different from mine; I had a relationship of sorts with Lance. It was more than limerence, deeper than a crush. Maybe it wasn't love, I don't know. Is there a name for that scenario?"

"I have never heard of it," Dirk said gently. "Come on, Cayenne, you know it was just a crush. People get them all the time. There is no shame in admitting it."

"If it was just a crush," Cayenne said, "I would have moved on long ago. I was seventeen when I met him, and I still think about him."

"Did you two have something serious?" Dirk asked incredulously. "Did you kiss, make out, have sex?"

"No, to all of the above," Cayenne said. "Maybe if we had done any of those things, I would have moved on; he would have disappointed me and broken my heart, but he stays in my head as a perfect specimen of manhood."

"What a position to be in, I wouldn't want to be the perfect specimen in any girl's thoughts. People on a pedestal are usually toppled," Dirk murmured. "I wonder what could account for your obsession. Did you go through childhood trauma? Have daddy issues?"

"Oh yes," Cayenne nodded. "All of the above."

"They say fixating on someone in an obsessive way can be a result of childhood trauma. You found someone to latch onto, to distract yourself from the pain."

"There was no pain," Cayenne traced the patterns on the lounge chair's armrest. "I don't remember what happened to me. What I heard about my childhood trauma was what my mother told me. I don't think my situation then had anything to do with my feelings for Lance."

"All our experiences are connected," Dirk said, "and child abuse can leave a mark whether you are aware of it or not. It's not surprising that you'd hold onto something—or someone—that made you feel good, even if it was just in your head."

Cayenne sighed. "I have had relationships since my unrequited limerence, crush, or whatever with Lance. It's not as if I put my life on pause and am actively pining over him."

"That's a relief," Dirk said softly. "Because I was about to feel really alarmed for you and the poor guy."

Cayenne laughed. "Don't be alarmed. It's just that what I felt for Lance was so unique, so special. I have always thought that if I can't repeat it with someone else, I won't marry."

"Oh my," Dirk whistled. "What did that Lance do to you to instigate such feelings?"

"He was great," Cayenne whispered. "Perfect."

"In what way?" Dirk asked, leaning in with genuine curiosity.

Cayenne's eyes softened as she delved into her memories. "He was everything I wanted in a person. He was kind and funny, always making me laugh. He was also incredibly smart, which made you feel inspired just listening to him. And he made everyone around him feel special like they were the only person in the room. And he listened to me. He really got me. I felt as if I didn't need words to convey my feelings."

Dirk nodded. "Sounds like quite a guy. But you know, nobody's perfect. Maybe you were seeing an idealized version of him."

Cayenne sighed, a wistful smile playing on her lips. "I know that, logically. But at seventeen, everything felt so intense and real."

"So, what happened? Why didn't anything come of it?" Dirk asked gently.

"He didn't see me that way," Cayenne admitted, her voice barely above a whisper. "I was just a kid, the pesky girl next door who would hound him at least once a day. Sometimes, he pretended he wasn't home to avoid me."

"Maybe because he was beginning to like you too and knew it wouldn't work," Dirk suggested.

"No," Cayenne sighed, "that's not it. I was really annoying. Looking back now, Lance had the patience of a saint. I would bring him food, volunteer to clean his house, question him about girls and who he liked, and tell him every single detail about my day. I would whine and complain about things that teenage girls whine and complain about. He would give me his undivided attention and offer advice."

Dirk chuckled.

"He never told me much about himself, though. He always brought the conversation around to me, and I was happy to do most of the talking. Of course, he wouldn't get away with that now. I would try to learn as much about him as I could. 'How old are you?' Cayenne sat up straighter in the chair.

"Twenty-seven," Dirk said.

And your birthday?" Dirk groaned. "March ninth."

"Oh," Cayenne slumped back in the chair, "Lance's birthday was July eleventh."

"So I guess we aren't twins then," Dirk exhaled.

"I guess so," Cayenne said sleepily. "What's your favorite color?"

"Green," Dirk said.

"His was yellow," Cayenne murmured. "What do you do in your spare time?"

"Are you comparing us?" Dirk asked gently.

"Yes, I am," Cayenne said. "I still think you are too similar to not be closely related."

Dirk laughed. "Well, then, in my spare time, I like to read both fiction and nonfiction. I am particularly fond of detective novels these days. I like a good 'whodunit' tale where I can't figure out who did it from the first chapter. I like photography and playing and watching cricket."

"Cool, I like cricket too!" Cayenne chuckled. "Lance liked photography. I got into the hobby because of him. I told you I was annoying. I know way more about taking pictures than I would have organically. And now I love it."

Dirk chuckled. "It's a great hobby, but I haven't taken up a camera in a while."

"Me neither," Cayenne murmured.

"So what do you do, Cayenne?" Dirk asked. "And what are your hobbies?"

"I am a hairdresser," Cayenne began, "when I graduated high school, I went to beauty school instead of college. My sister Cinnamon made a big deal out of it, so I promised her that I would get a degree. So I did, part-time. I had my own shop and was doing my own thing for two years. Then, I met a client at a fundraiser who told me that Lookbook Hair and Spa had an empty chair and asked if I was interested?"

"Of course, I was interested!" Cayenne chuckled. "I had to interview with Tony Ray. He doesn't allow just anyone to work at his place."

"Tony Ray, stylist to the stars, I saw the ads he had out a couple of years ago," Dirk said. "You work for that guy?"

"That's right," Cayenne nodded. "And I love it. We have profit-sharing. I don't have to pay my own shop rent, buy supplies, or do any of the administrative work that comes with owning your own thing. I show up for work, I have all state-of-the-art equipment, and I get to focus on my clients and my craft. It's a dream come true. Plus, the networking opportunities are incredible. I've met so many influential people there; my client list is literally the 'who's who' in Jamaica."

"Wow, that sounds amazing," Dirk said, genuinely impressed. "So, do you see yourself staying there long term?"

"Definitely," Cayenne replied. "I am in no hurry to go on my own again. Besides, I like my co-workers; they are like family. You do know we are a full-service outfit, don't you? For both males and females. You can stop by."

"I'll consider it," Dirk said. "I haven't been to a barber in years. I trim my own hair. I remember my dad and I would have our male bonding time together at the shop, and then we'd stop at the bakery and pick up my favorite treat. Good times."

"I thought you said your father was dead," Cayenne said.

"My biological father is," Dirk said. "My mother's husband is my dad."

"Oh," Cayenne murmured. "Lance never mentioned his family much. He spoke about his mother several times; he had young siblings. I think she had a baby while he was house-sitting next door. He said he seized the opportunity to house-sit because the baby kept crying, and he could hear the cries from the pool house."

"So we are back to Lance?" Dirk sighed. "I am telling you, Cayenne, I am about to have a complex."

"If you met Lance, you would know why I am baffled by you," Cayenne sighed. "What did you do your masters in?"

"Who said I have a master's?" Dirk asked.

"Well, do you?" Cayenne asked.

"Let's say I don't," Dirk sighed. "I assume Lance had his master's."

"He did," Cayenne said thoughtfully.

Dirk leaned back. "I am not him, Cayenne."

"I'll only agree if I see you both in a room together," Cayenne said. "I should look him up. I wonder what he is doing right now…"

Her voice petered off.

"Cayenne," Dirk whispered, but he heard a snuffle, deep breathing; she was out for the count.

Dirk grimaced in the dark. The last thing he wanted right now was for Cayenne to break his cover. But how would he walk the tightrope of investigating Alex and not letting his feelings for Cayenne be involved? He got up as stealthily as possible and returned to his side of the patio. He would be working extra hard to tie up this case. He wanted to tell Cayenne the truth about himself, and he wanted to do it soon.

Chapter Eight

It seemed as if everyone slept late. By the time Cayenne reached the cavernous kitchen at ten, breakfast was just being served. Dirk was already there, sitting beside Alex. Cayenne glanced at him and then at her friend. She was dressed to the nines in a floating negligee with a face full of makeup. Cayenne repressed her grin and sat beside Anton.

"Ah, it's Cayenne," Sanya announced, "she slept on the patio last night! Sorry, girl."

"I had a good time," Cayenne said, sitting down. "I had no issues. I woke up this morning thankful that it was overcast because I would be fried by now."

Anton winked, "You should come and sleep in my room. You can turn the temperature as low as you want and then cuddle up to me."

The rest of the group laughed, except Dirk. He was looking between the two of them, curiosity in his gaze.

"Nothing to see here," Cayenne felt compelled to say,

"just Anton being his usual thirsty self."

Why was she even clarifying the situation for Dirk? She didn't know.

"And I will be thirsty until you give some attention," Anton said. "Now, Cayenne, what do you expect of me? Should I stand in the middle of the road and let something run over me, so that I can get your full attention?"

"Why on earth would she give you attention?" Alex piped in. "You change girlfriends like the brake pads on your broke-down car."

"If it isn't the pot calling me a kettle," Anton said cheekily, "watch out for her, Dirk. Her track record is just like mine."

"That is so not true," Alex widened her eyes. "Somebody defend me!"

"Let's talk about the weather," Sanya said.

There were chuckles all around.

"I can't believe this," Alex looked around the table. "Cayenne, you are my best friend. Say something."

"The weather is nice out today," Cayenne said, taking a bite out of a grapefruit slice. "I like that it's not too hot and humid."

"It's perfect for sailing," Alex took the hint and changed the topic. "My boss, well Dirk's boss too, has a yacht, and he invited all of us to a party he is having today. His yacht is large, so he'll send some small boats to pick us up from the jetty."

"What in the luxury?" Sanya whistled. "I am in total awe!"

"Be ready by one, everybody. We'll sail to Portland, where he picks up a friend. Then we'll go to a private cove to swim and snorkel, and then he'll drop us off here and head back to Kingston."

Cayenne raised her brows. Alex and her boss, Stephen, were unusually close these days. In the cog that was LAD

Wealth Management, Alex was suddenly elevated to being invited to parties on yachts.

"Your boss?" Anton widened his eyes. "We are going to party with your boss? How did you score that?"

"I told him I would be in the vicinity with some friends, and he said, well, join the party! I'll stop and pick you up. He especially wants to meet you, Cayenne."

"Me?" Cayenne widened her eyes.

"I talk about you a lot; he knows your father," Alex said.

"Not interested in any of my father's friends," Cayenne murmured.

She glanced at Dirk and realized he was frowning, and then their eyes met.

"How do you feel about partying with your boss?" Cayenne asked him.

"It will be a real privilege and an honor to schmooze. Stephen has always struck me as a cool guy," Dirk said lightly. "And I assume there will be other heavy hitters at this party."

"Oh yes," Alex said excitedly. "So put your game faces on and be nice."

"I am going to get our business cards," Kinsley told Tessa. We'll have to make this work."

Tessa nodded. "We'll work this, babe."

"Whatever you do, none of you embarrass me," Alex said. "I am not just talking to Kinsley and Tessa, all of you. Don't be thirsty and hound the rich people! We'll party until sunset, then come back here and relax for a bit, and then we'll party some more. There's a barefoot on the beach party beginning at eleven tonight at the beach club."

"I don't know if I have the stamina for that," Sanya said. "Being in water usually tires me."

"I was about to say the same thing," Cayenne rolled her

eyes. "I am here chiefly because I wanted to relax over the long weekend. I am on my feet all day as a hairdresser. I was looking for activities more on the lounging side this weekend."

"All of us are in our twenties," Alex said. "You do these things while you're still young. You're up for an adventure, aren't you, Dirk?"

Dirk nodded. "I am, but within reason. It depends on how tired I feel when we get back."

"Those are my sentiments, too," Anton said. "I am juggling two jobs at the moment. One party a day is just about as much as I can take with two jobs. I do have student loans to pay back."

"Don't we all," Sanya said. "Well, all of us except Cayenne, who had the foresight to work and then go to college part-time. She graduated late, but she did it."

"Cayenne is not the only student loan-free person in here. I paid off mine," Alex said boastfully.

"You did?" Sanya widened her eyes.

"One of the first things I did," Alex said. "When I made some money."

"That's it," Sanya joked. "I am applying for a job at LAD Wealth. Not only did you get a major promotion in record time, but you could pay off your student loans, buy a new car, move into the Wilde Building, and vacation like a rock star, and your boss is coming to pick you up with a yacht! I envy you."

"Dirk, are you swimming in money like Alex?" Sanya asked.

"I, uh," Dirk looked up from his plate. "I, um, I don't think so."

"Dirk is not a wealth manager," Alex laughed. "He is in accounts."

"That's right," Dirk nodded. "The rock stars are the people who make the investment decisions. I am just your humble paper pusher, hired to ensure all figures are in order and everyone gets paid on time. No yachts for me."

"Oh, come on, Dirk," Alex said, gazing at him with adoration. "You do more than just push papers. Without you, the rest of us wouldn't know our profit margins from our expense accounts. You're the backbone of the operation."

Cayenne looked between him and Alex. Something was not right. More was going on beneath the surface than what was before her eyes. Exactly what it was? She didn't quite know. But she had a niggling feeling that Alex was in trouble and Dirk's visit was not just a casual weekend hang out with friends.

Chapter Nine

Stephen's yacht was named Bodacious; it was a stunning vessel that made quite an impact as it approached. It boasted three levels: the lower deck housed the engine room and crew quarters, the main deck featured an expansive salon and a gourmet kitchen, and the upper deck boasted a luxurious master suite with panoramic ocean views. Each level was elegantly designed with polished wood finishes and state-of-the-art technology.

When they stepped aboard, they were greeted by a crew dressed in crisp white uniforms, ready to cater to their every need. The atmosphere was vibrant and filled with anticipation.

"Welcome aboard, everyone!" Stephen's cheerful voice boomed from the upper deck, where he stood with a glass of champagne. "Make yourselves at home. Today is all about relaxation and celebration!"

Cayenne was in awe of the sheer opulence surrounding

her. The salon was a perfect blend of comfort and style, with plush seating and large windows that offered breathtaking views of the sea. The panoramic view was even more stunning than she had imagined, with the sea stretching out endlessly, the horizon blending seamlessly with the clear blue sky.

"Now this," Alex said, linking her arms with Cayenne's, "is how you start a fabulous weekend."

Cayenne laughed, feeling the cool breeze on her face and the rhythm of the music in her veins. "I could get used to this."

"Me too," Alex said, "this is our song."

"Life is the greatest gift given to humanity, surround yourself with a lot of positive energy," Alex sang along with the song, grinning widely. They did a little dance together, drawing the attention of the rest of the group.

Stephen joined the group and clapped when they finished. He was a handsome biracial man in his early fifties, with piercing brown eyes and a warm, inviting smile that made everyone feel at ease.

His salt-and-pepper hair added to his distinguished appearance, giving him an air of wisdom and experience. Dressed in a crisp white linen shirt and tailored navy shorts, he exuded a casual elegance that matched the sophistication of his yacht.

"I should ask the DJ to replay the song. I welcome Alex's friends! Today, I am not a boss, just a humble seaman who wants you to have a good time."

He introduced himself to everyone and shook hands with them all. He paused in front of Dirk and then shook his hand.

"If it isn't the face that launches a thousand ships. All the women in LAD Wealth are crazy about this guy!"

Dirk smiled.

"Okay, let me give you all a tour," Stephen said. "I have had this boat for four months. This is her second voyage."

He guided them through the yacht and enthusiastically spoke about its design and the adventures he wanted to experience aboard Bodacious. He was approachable and fun, and Cayenne's doubts about him showing special favors to Alex eased.

"The question is," Sanya sidled up to her and whispered, "Is he married?"

Alex heard and glared at Sanya. "He is divorced twice, but he has a girlfriend. That lady over there." She pointed to a voluptuous woman standing at the bow of the boat in a string bikini. Anton was heading toward the girl.

"Oh no," Alex groaned. "I can't invite him anywhere. Let me go avert a crisis. I don't want Stephen to kick us all off; we haven't started our adventure yet." Alex walked over to Anton and whispered fiercely to him. He stopped in his tracks and looked around sheepishly.

Sanya laughed. "I swear his tongue was out. You know your friend Dirk didn't once glance at her? All the guys did when they walked up to this deck. Some gave her a second and a third look, but he wasn't even moved."

"Really?" Cayenne looked at Sanya.

"Really," Sanya nodded. "I don't think he is interested in Alex either. I see him looking at you when he thinks no one is looking. I've been hyper-vigilant. Someone should give me a detective badge already. I think I know what is going on."

"You do?" Cayenne whispered.

"I do," Sanya nodded. "And it's epic."

"What's epic?" Alex asked.

"Did I say epic?" Sanya shook her head. "I meant I am going to have to take a pic. My family won't believe this unless I do."

"She's strange," Alex said when Sanya walked away. "She has gotten stranger with time. Maybe we should drop her from the friend group."

"Don't say that," Cayenne whispered.

"I am planning to phase out most of them," Alex said. "Anton and Sanya, for sure. They are embarrassing, always discussing the cost of things and moaning about student loans and second jobs." She linked her arm with Cayenne's. "Anyway, I'll do that at another time. Isn't this exciting? We are going to St. Thomas. There is a mile of beach there that is pure white sand. There, we will swim, snorkel, relax, and then go down the coast to a private villa in Port Antonio. Stephen's friend is famous, Carlos Guthrie, the financier."

"This is glorious, Cayenne. We are living the life we have always dreamed of, vacations in luxury villas, partying on a yacht."

"Come on, let's go say hi to Stephen privately. He said he wants to talk to you."

"But why?" Cayenne was confused.

Stephen was on the upper deck. They passed through the salon, which was bustling with laughter and conversation. There were people gathered in clusters with drinks in hand, everyone dressed in some form of bathing suit or pull-over. The sea breeze was vigorous. It had snatched the straw hat she had worn over her ponytail several times. She finally took it off and put it in her bag.

The gourmet kitchen was a hub of activity. The aroma of freshly baked bread and grilled seafood wafted through the air, mingling with the salty sea breeze.

She surreptitiously looked for Dirk, who was in lively conversation with an older man. He saw her looking and waved.

She snapped her head around quickly.

Stephen smiled when he saw them coming. "Would you like a glass of wine?" he asked Cayenne. "It is Valerian Jet, their newest wine. I understand your mother was the one who developed it and named it after your nephew."

"No thanks," Cayenne said, "I am not much of a drinker."

"For shame, and you are a Greystone!" Stephen chuckled. How ironic that a granddaughter of the leading winemaker in the Caribbean has no taste for alcohol."

She glanced at Alex. So that is why he was interested in her? He thought she was one of the Greystones!

"I only recently found out my mother was related to them," Cayenne said quickly. "I am not one of the key Greystones. I have nothing to do with the wine business. I am just a hairdresser."

"I know that," Stephen laughed. "Cayenne Onyx Aubry. I have known you since you were a speck in your mother's eye. I am your kin. Your cousin. We share the same grandmother."

"Alex, leave us," he turned to her friend, who had been silent until then. I have some family history to discuss with Cayenne."

Alex nodded. "Well, see you downstairs."

"I know your mother does not want anything to do with the Aubrys, and she has kept you and Sage away," Stephen said. "Believe me, I understand it. We are a messed up bunch."

Cayenne gasped. "I didn't know you were an Aubry."

"Yes, I am," Stephen nodded, "by my mother's side. How much of the Aubry family tree do you know?"

"Nothing, really. I know my mother married my father when she was eighteen, and he was forty-two," Cayenne shrugged. "He was a sculptor and used her as his muse. That's the extent of it."

Stephen nodded. "Well, we are a small family. Your father's parents are Dean and Rosa Aubry. They had three children: your father, Paul; my mother, Donna; and an uncle, Horace."

"Paul, as you know, is in jail. He had you and Sage. My mother had me and my sisters Anita and Jill, and Horace had three sons. They are the exception to the messed-up rule. They are all doing well."

"Good to know," Cayenne said.

"We were all close at one-time," Stephen cleared his throat. "My sisters and I spent summers with Uncle Paul when we were younger. He would disappear with one or both of them at a time. I had no idea why. We were all under ten years old. My sister Jill was five, and Anita was seven. After a while, my mother stopped us from going by him, and I never understood why."

"No one told me what was going on. I did not know why the family didn't invite him over anymore. I didn't know anything," Stephen sighed. "So I naively sought him out when I was older. You see, to me, he had been the fun uncle who took me fishing and taught me to ride a bike. When I looked him up, he was married to your mom, and she had just found out she was pregnant with you."

Cayenne tensed up, knowing where this was going.

"I reported my happy findings to my family," Stephen said. "Needless to say, nobody was happy to hear. My mother started to cry. My sisters clammed up and looked shifty, and then I got the whole story. Uncle Paul was a pedophile. When he disappeared with my sisters when we visited, he was molesting them."

Cayenne sat down. "Wow."

"He had been terrorizing young girls in our community unchecked for years. His parents knew about it and did nothing; other well-thinking community members turned a blind eye. The Aubry's were rich, and Paul could get away with it. Whenever he raped one of the girls in the community, they paid off the parents to shut up. He never messed with anyone of means.

"And when our grandfather died, he quite inexplicably left all of his wealth to Paul. Our grandmother got the house and a stipend, but everything went to that monster. And with that power, he had no qualms about setting his sights on his own family.

"He paid off his sister to shut up about what her girls said he did to them. And my mother took the money and stayed silent. I find it hard not to judge my mother about that even though my mother was broke as a church mouse, my father was a gambler, you see, and she was all but destitute. My father had squandered her small inheritance from Grandpa Dean. That's why she sent us to Uncle Paul for the summers and lunch money."

"Oh," Cayenne cleared her throat. "So sorry to hear. Where's your dad now?"

"Dead." Stephen said, "No condolences necessary. He was caught stealing, and the homeowner shot him. After he died, Uncle Paul became the sole financier of our family."

"And that's why your mother did nothing to avenge your sisters' abuse," Cayenne said.

"That's right," Stephen sighed. "It doesn't matter how long ago it was. He left quite an impact on my sisters. They are both messed up. They are trying to beat addictions, and not one of them can have a steady relationship to save her life. I want to think that Uncle Paul did that, but I am on my third potential marriage. Who am I going to blame for that? He never molested me."

Cayenne blinked rapidly. "I had no clue about any of this."

"I told your mother when you were a baby about Uncle Paul," Stephen said. "She was pregnant with Sage at the time. I don't know what she did with the information, but apparently, she watched him like a hawk."

Cayenne nodded.

"Well," Stephen sighed, "I wonder what she will do when he is released? I heard it could be any day now. They are letting him loose early for good behavior. His psychiatrist and spiritual advisor declare him cured."

"What?" Cayenne was stunned. "I didn't know he would be released so early!"

Stephen nodded. "Scum like him should have gotten the death penalty, but he is about to walk free. He deserves to be punished in every way there is. When he comes out, do not go near him."

"You don't have to tell me that twice," Cayenne said. "I… this is shocking."

"Sorry," Stephen said grimly.

"I would have found out anyway," Cayenne shrugged.

"I don't want you to think about it," Stephen said earnestly. "Have fun today; eat, drink, and frolic with your friends. Alex is an exceptional young woman, a good friend to have."

Cayenne nodded.

"I have been meaning to approach you ever since I started working at LAD. I saw you in the parking lot with Alex, but then I said let me leave things as they are. What's past is past. But your father's imminent return made me think I should tell you the truth of things."

"Thank you for letting me know," Cayenne nodded.

Stephen raised his glass to her and headed below deck.

Cayenne stood up and looked at the azure waters unseeingly. She was no longer in a party mood. Hearing about her father had soured things for her. She couldn't deny that it was a glorious day, the type of day to feel light and carefree, but instead, she felt burdened by what she just heard, and a dark depression enveloped her.

Chapter Ten

"If you frown any fiercer, you'll start scaring away the sunshine," Dirk teased. "Why are you glaring at the sea like that?"

Cayenne was standing unusually still and staring at the sea. He had been watching her while she spoke to Stephen and afterward, as she stood mulling over their conversation. He gave her five minutes, but she was still standing where he had last seen her, a scowl on her face. This was introverted behavior, and he knew that Cayenne was no introvert. She was a people person, and they were playing all her favorite songs. He had expected her to come down to the main deck, dance, and chat her way through the small crowd.

Stephen must have said something to upset her, he thought. He wanted to know what it was. He was curious about Stephen and Alex's connection, too. He felt as if he was near a breakthrough in the case.

"I didn't realize I was frowning," Cayenne looked over her

shoulder and offered him a wan smile. "I was just thinking. I have a lot to think about."

"Like what?" Dirk stood beside her.

"Stuff," Cayenne shrugged.

"Was Stephen propositioning you?" Dirk asked jealously.

"God no," Cayenne shook her head. "He is actually my cousin. My father is his uncle. He just explained to me why my father's side of the family isn't close, and I am a bit shell-shocked. I don't know why I should be, but I am. He also said my father will be released from prison any day now. I didn't know that; it's just sinking in."

Dirk knew all about Paul Aubry's crimes against Cayenne and Sage, but that was when he was Lance. He inhaled. He should not know what they were now, so he had to ask to make this authentic.

"Your father is in prison?"

"Yes," Cayenne looked at him. "Remember when I told you I was abused as a child?"

"I do. Last night, I asked if you had daddy issues or were abused, and you said all of the above. I did not pry further because I figured it would have been sensitive information."

"Well, it is, but I was so young, I don't remember," Cayenne shrugged. "My father was the worst kind of abuser; he had an inappropriate fixation on children. Stephen just told me about other victims in the family. It's too much."

"He should have gotten life in prison," Dirk said feelingly.

"That's the same thing that Stephen said," Cayenne grimaced. "I wonder how my mom is going to take his imminent release. She is in such a good space right now. She has a good job and a long-running relationship with a guy who genuinely likes her, and she is happy, maybe for the first time in her life. This is going to derail her."

"It doesn't have to derail her once he keeps out of her

way," Dirk said. "When he gets out, where is he going to go?"

"To one of his houses, I suppose," Cayenne said. "He is a rich man, you know. I doubt prison has put a stop to that. As Stephen has so bitterly pointed out, he inherited quite a bit from his father. He had several properties and investments; he even had investments set up for me and Sage while in prison. When his lawyer contacted my mother to tell her the good news, my mother told him to shove the investment where the sun didn't shine."

"Your mother sounds fierce," Dirk chuckled.

"She is. She has been through a lot," Cayenne sighed.

"And so have you," Dirk said, "and I am pretty sure she wouldn't want you to be at a boat party allowing thoughts of your father to darken your life. Get up, join the fray, and be your bubbly, sunny self. There'll be time enough to think about your father getting out of prison."

Cayenne smiled. "You think I am sunny!"

"I do," Dirk nodded, "that's our song playing. We should dance together."

Cayenne laughed. "Kelissa and Chronixx's song 'Winner' is our song?"

"Yep," Dirk held out his hand. "Listen to the words, 'If I am living, I have to live it up, no matter the feeling, I have to get up.' It's as if they are singing it just for you."

Cayenne smiled. "I will have to tell the DJ to replay this," Dirk said as they headed down the stairs. He held onto her hand and went over to the booth, whispering to the DJ. He did indeed play it, and Cayenne danced with Dirk while singing happily, "You are a winner; oh, you can get through it!" They were oblivious to Alex's fulsome glares.

Dirk didn't leave her side much after that. He had his motives; he loved spending time with Cayenne and didn't want to see her down and depressed.

They were at the cove, a picturesque place nestled between rocky cliffs that rose from the shoreline. He was taking a brief break from the water; Cayenne was learning how to snorkel and having a whale of a time doing it. He was feeling a bit drowsy. The white sand felt silky underfoot, and the cove's waters reflected the sky's brilliant blue.

Alex passed him by and stopped, casting a shadow over his legs. "You have been avoiding me."

"I have not," Dirk said lazily.

"You were hanging out with Cayenne and ignoring me," Alex crouched beside him. "I thought you came this weekend so that we can get to know each other better."

"I was making sure she was okay," Dirk said. "After talking to Stephen, she was a bit down."

"Oh yeah," Alex nodded. "He said he'd tell her they were related and that I should not say it until he did."

"When did you know that they were related?" Dirk asked.

"Six months ago," Alex said. "I was going to lunch with Cayenne, and he was going to a meeting. He saw her in the parking lot. He called me to his office the day after and…"

"And?" Dirk asked.

"That's it," Alex shrugged. "Let's talk about something else. Something that has nothing to do with work or Cayenne."

Dirk sat up straighter. Six months ago, Alex suddenly got her promotion and started rolling in money. What was the connection? He would have to take a closer look at all the accounts she was actively working on and search for a connection with Cayenne.

"So, what do you want to do tonight?" Alex asked lazily. "We could go to the beach party or snuggle up with a glass of wine, chat in my room, or watch a movie."

Dirk glanced at Alex. He wanted to go home and sift through her files. An idea was forming in his head. How was he going to get away?

"I think I am leaving tonight," he answered Alex.

"But why?" Alex asked crestfallen. "You just got here; we have one more day tomorrow. I hoped we could carve out some time just you and me…"

"That was fun," Sanya said, interrupting them and sitting down. "You should try it, Alex."

"I am having a conversation here," Alex growled. "Scoot! Go away!"

"Well, excuse me," Sanya got up quickly. "Sorry!"

Cayenne was on her way toward them, and Sanya shook her head. 'She is grumpy, stay away!'"

Dirk chuckled when Cayenne stopped and then started walking backward toward the sea.

Alex glared at him. "You like her, don't you?"

"I do," Dirk admitted.

"But you just met her!" Alex said. "I can't believe this!"

"Keep your voice down, Alex," Dirk said. "We are attracting attention."

Alex got up and glared at him. "You are going to regret choosing Cayenne over me."

"I didn't choose her over you…" he was arguing with himself; Alex was speed-walking away.

Chapter Eleven

Alex glared at her for most of the day, and Cayenne had no idea why. She had backed away from Alex and Dirk when they were talking and given them their space, so in her opinion, this hostility was uncalled for.

Alex had even made it a point to sit at the opposite end of the boat that took them in from her. They had boarded the small boat, all girls in one and all guys in the other. When they alighted at the jetty, Alex had quickly walked ahead of them and into the house in a huff.

"What's gotten into her?" Iris asked out loud.

"She is acting like someone stole her man," Tessa giggled. "Which one of you is the culprit, Sanya, Cayenne? You are the only single girls here."

"Not me," Sanya said, "all I did today was suggest that Alex join us in snorkeling. She ran me like a dog. Cayenne was laughing and chatting with Dirk before we reached the cove."

"I was trying to get into the party mood. Dirk was just being friendly," Cayenne said. She looked behind her; the boat with Dirk and the other guys was coming in. "Maybe it's something Dirk said; maybe we should ask him."

"I am not that interested in your little drama," Tessa shrugged. "I am going to go to my room, shower, and sleep until the morning. Today was fun; I still feel as if I am in the water. And my belly is wonderfully full. Nighty night, girls. I love you lots; you can let me know how it goes tomorrow when Alex blows her top."

"I have never seen Alex jealous before," Iris said in wonder, "even when she was dating Joey and he became interested in me, she was cool with it."

Kehlani yawned behind them, "I am going to follow Tessa's example and go to bed. There is something about the sea and how it laps against you that makes me sleepy. I am going to hit the showers before Noah, though. Update me in the morning."

"She has a point about the shower," Sanya said, "race you to the shower, Cayenne."

Cayenne started running. She barely made it before Sanya. She showered quickly, washed the salt from her hair, and changed into a red summer dress. She used her Denman brush to create corkscrew curls on her mid-back-length hair. It would air dry quickly; there was a nice breeze outside.

She stood on the patio with her nose in the air.

"You look gorgeous," Sanya said behind her, admiring Cayenne's glowing skin and long curly hair. "I didn't know your hair was that long. Tell me exactly what you do so that I can replicate it."

Cayenne looked around at her. "Thanks, Sanya. Haven't we had this conversation before?"

"Maybe," Sanya said sheepishly. "I vaguely recall you

telling me not to bleach my hair and relax it on the same day."

"Your hair will grow after your last cut," Cayenne said. "That's what hair does, it grows. Give it time and treat it right."

"Yes, ma'am, you are the expert," Sanya said. "I was considering switching hairdressers and coming to your salon, but you guys are too expensive. Besides, I told you already that I cannot make it so far across town on a weekday."

"And I told you already that you should call me on the weekend whenever you are ready; I can do your hair at my house," Cayenne reminded her.

Sanya nodded. "Well, now that I have destroyed all my hair cuticles, I think I may have to take you up on that offer."

Cayenne laughed.

"Ladies, I heard your voices and didn't want to leave without saying goodbye," Dirk said as he came outside, freshly showered and fully dressed in black. He looked handsome and charismatic, exuding an air of effortless confidence.

"I see what you see," Sanya whispered to Cayenne. "But I understand Alex's anger, too. That is one fine man, and he doesn't like her as much as he does you."

Cayenne cleared her throat. "I thought you were spending the weekend."

"Something came up," Dirk said. "It was a pleasure meeting both of you…"

Alex stepped behind him with a scowl. "It's your fault why he is leaving, Cayenne!"

"Me?" Cayenne squealed. "What did I do?"

"Now, Alex," Dirk said quietly, "I told you this has nothing to do with Cayenne."

"It does," Alex hopped over the low balcony wall and headed for Cayenne.

Cayenne took a step back. She was genuinely frightened of Alex. She looked like she would push her over the balustrade. Dirk must have thought the same; he came after Alex.

"You are a man-stealer; I didn't expect it of you," Alex growled. "I actually can't believe it! You know I like Dirk! Why couldn't you fade into the background for once? You know you are not a normal woman!"

"What?" Cayenne frowned.

"Can we not have this conversation, Alex?" Dirk asked.

"No," Alex glared at him. "I invited you to be with me for the weekend, but you gave my friend all the attention. I saw the way you two were dancing and how you touched her today. And your little giggly fest. I know you like her, but guess what? It's all for naught; Cayenne cannot be intimate with anyone. So if you were hoping that something would come of this, you are in for a surprise, buddy."

"Wait a minute," Cayenne gasped, "what are you talking about, Alex?"

"I read your father's court records," Alex said spitefully, "he destroyed your female parts when he molested you. The doctor said you couldn't function normally as an adult. You wouldn't have any sensory abilities."

"They had to do reconstruction surgery down there on you, and they removed your ovaries. Technically, you are a female eunuch. Didn't your mother tell you? Haven't you ever questioned why you haven't had sex with anyone? Or even want to? You are not really a woman. At this point, your personal pronoun should be they or them."

There was a collective gasp from Cayenne, Sanya, and Dirk.

Cayenne opened her mouth and then closed it. You could hear a pin drop after that declaration. "None of this is true," Cayenne's voice sounded like it was coming from far away. There was a roaring in her ears.

She backed away from Alex's snarling face; she felt like she was moving in molasses. "That's a very mean thing to say," Sanya said to Alex. "Even if it's true, why would you say that in front of people? She is your best friend. When you found that out, you should take her aside quietly and ask her what the deal is."

Alex turned to Sanya and glared at her. "As of now, I have no friends. And that includes you. You are a penny-pinching, pocket-watching, money-grubbing hanger-on who is always judging people on their spending habits but quite quick to jump on the gravy train. You have no right to speak to me about anything. Beggars keep their broke-mouth shut!"

Sanya blinked rapidly. "Wow. Tell me how you really feel, Alex. Say, Dirk, can I get a lift with you into Kingston? I don't want to be a hanger-on for one minute more."

Dirk nodded. Cayenne was standing there in shock. "Do you need a lift, too, Cayenne? I know you came with Alex."

Cayenne nodded. Her tongue was not working. She glanced at Alex's snarling face and then the entrance to the room; she needed to put one foot in front of the other, walk to the room, and start packing, but her mind was working overtime. When had Alex read her father's court files? Why didn't she know about how badly abused she had been? Her mother always said she had stopped things before it got too far.

She was fine down there! She really was. She knew her own body; she had been pleasing herself for years. She was sensitive and functioning.

And so what if she didn't sleep around? She had to feel

something for someone first. That did not mean she was a female eunuch.

She hadn't had reconstructive surgery? Or had she? She didn't know!

She moved toward the room, and her steps faltered.

"Keep going," Dirk said beside her. "I'll take your bags to the car."

Cayenne looked across at him; he was blurry. Then she realized that she had tears in her eyes. And then they started to fall, and the tears wouldn't stop. Dirk hugged her to him while she whimpered; she couldn't even sob properly. The feeling at the bottom of her stomach was too complex, heavy, and painful.

"Oh my God, I am so sorry, I said that," Alex said behind them. "I was angry. I was jealous. I am sorry, Cayenne. Please forgive me."

"I'll pack her things," Sanya said from the doorway. "I don't know how you are going to come back from this, Alex; you really used a child abuse victim issues as an argument because of jealousy? That's low."

Chapter Twelve

"**Y**ou are investigating Alex, aren't you?" Sanya asked Dirk after they had been driving for a while.

Cayenne had cried herself to sleep. After her crying jag, she had docilely entered the car and curled up in the back seat, using her bag as a pillow.

Dirk looked back at her to ensure she was still sleeping because Sanya was looking at him knowingly. Dirk glanced at Sanya; her question had come out of left field.

"I am still trying to digest what Alex said about Cayenne," he answered, trying to deflect from her question.

"I don't believe it," Sanya said. "I don't think she is a female eunuch. She may have gotten reconstructive surgery, yes, for certain damages, but I doubt she is smooth as a doll down there or that she lost her clitoris. That's where the majority of the sensation is for females."

Dirk nodded. "I know that."

"Oh my goodness, do you think she lost it?" Sanya asked.

"If she did, then that would have been bad damage. And to remove her ovaries. My god, her father should be hanged."

Dirk glanced at Sanya. "I am trying not to think of Cayenne's ovaries or clitoris."

"Oh, come on, that's all anyone can think about right now," Sanya said. "I watched a documentary once about female genital mutilation, and the statistics are mind-boggling. Right now, in the twenty-first century, over two hundred million women are mutilated. There was one particular lady who they interviewed; she said they practiced it in her tribe so that women could be pure for marriage and keep them from straying because it suppresses sexual desires. They had it done as a tribal ritual from when she was a baby. They sliced off…"

"Okay, you got me," Dirk interrupted Sanya. "I was investigating Alex."

Sanya smiled. "I knew it. It wasn't hard to put it together; I consider myself an amateur detective. I was going to bust your secret to Cayenne this evening, but then you came onto the patio, and this happened."

"There is no secret," Dirk said. "Alex came up on the radar, and I am just following the crumbs. I am happy you didn't say anything. You would have hampered my investigation."

"Sorry," Sanya said sheepishly. "I would have just told Cayenne."

"And she may have told Alex," Dirk glanced in the back. "Can you please not say anything? I am quite close to figuring this out."

"Of course," Sanya nodded. "I'll keep my mouth shut. Alex deserves whatever is coming to her because she embarrassed Cayenne like that. Imagine you live your whole life not knowing that you are butchered down there, and then your best friend blurts it out in front of a guy the both of you are interested in. Whew, that was too much.

"But that was mission accomplished; she wanted to tell you that. She wanted you to never be interested in Cayenne because of it. Alex is diabolical."

"Who says I won't be interested in Cayenne?" Dirk asked.

"Well, I assumed she'd go straight to the friend zone after this. I mean, you obviously like her, but she can't be a sexual partner."

Dirk sighed. "We'll cross that bridge when we get to it."

Sanya snorted. "You are going to ditch her. You are a man; you have needs. Please don't act all noble and string Cayenne along, thinking you can handle a sexless existence. Don't break my friend's heart. She liked one guy who looked like you before; she doesn't need to be dropped by another. I remember when Lance left without telling her goodbye she talked about it for the whole year. If you are going to cut her loose, be honest with her and tell her you can't see yourself with someone with her limitations. Give her a proper goodbye."

Dirk inhaled. "She was quite into Lance, wasn't she?"

"Oh yes," Sanya said. "Maybe it's for the best he left before they could get intimate. Can you imagine the embarrassment when she found out she couldn't get aroused or that her downstairs wasn't functioning and may be made of rubber? What do they make fake vulvas with, do you know?"

"Okay, that's it," Dirk looked at Sanya. "Can we please not have a conversation about Cayenne's... situation? It's making me quite uncomfortable."

"Okay, my lips are sealed." Sanya gestured an imaginary zip over her lips. "Do you want to tell me about your real job?"

"I am a forensic auditor," Dirk said. "I am hired when there's suspicion of financial misconduct, fraud, or embezzlement within a company. My job is to dig deep into financial records, trace irregular transactions, and uncover the truth behind shady activities. It's like being a detective but for numbers."

Sanya raised an eyebrow. "So, you're a financial Sherlock Holmes?"

Dirk chuckled. "You could say that. It's not as glamorous as it sounds, though. Most of the time, it's long hours pouring over spreadsheets and trying to make sense of complex financial trails. But it can be rewarding, especially when you catch the bad guys."

"Wow," Sanya said, genuinely impressed. "I'd love to do something like that. I am good with numbers and detecting discrepancies. What degrees do I need?"

"Well, you'd need a strong accounting and finance foundation. Forensic auditors have at least a bachelor's degree in accounting, finance, or a related field. Some even pursue a master's degree to deepen their knowledge and improve their career prospects."

Sanya nodded, listening intently. "I have my bachelor's in economics."

"Good," Dirk nodded. "But education alone isn't enough. You'll also need certifications. The most recognized ones are the Certified Fraud Examiner (CFE) and Certified Public Accountant (CPA). Each of these has its own requirements and exams, but they're crucial if you want to be taken seriously in this field."

"That sounds intense," Sanya said, her excitement undeterred. "But I like a challenge. How did you get started?"

"I worked for a company specializing in forensic accounting for a few years, then pursued the CFE certification. It involved a lot of studying, but it was worth it. Real-world experience is also key. I learned a lot on the job, working with seasoned professionals and handling cases."

"That makes sense," Sanya said thoughtfully. "It's a mix of education, certifications, and practical experience."

"Exactly," Dirk confirmed. "And don't underestimate the importance of soft skills. It would help if you were detail-oriented, analytical, and persistent. Good communication skills are also crucial because you'll often have to explain your findings to people who might not have a finance background."

"Cool, how much does it pay?"

Dirk smiled. "It depends on various factors like your experience level, the region you work in, and the type of employer. Entry-level positions might start around $50,000 to $60,000 a year, but with experience and certifications, you can easily make six figures."

Sanya's eyes widened. "Really? That's impressive. I had no idea forensic auditors could make that much."

"Yeah, it's a well-paying field, especially if you work for major corporations, government agencies, or consulting firms," Dirk said. "And if you go the private investigator route and work high-profile cases, the pay can be even higher."

"Sounds like there's a lot of room for growth," Sanya remarked.

"There is," Dirk agreed. "Plus, the demand for forensic auditors is on the rise as financial regulations get stricter and businesses become more aware of the need to protect themselves from fraud."

"That's good to know," Sanya said. "Thanks, Dirk. You've given me a lot to think about."

"Anytime," Dirk replied. "You seem to have a knack for it. You knew what I was about in less than a day."

"That's because I felt something wasn't right with Alex and

her spending habits lately. I work in payroll, I am just junior staff, but I have a broad idea of salaries at the bank where I work, and we pay at the higher end of the average. And I know what a senior wealth manager's salary would be. I just put two and two together. Alex didn't win the lottery and had no surprise inheritance; things didn't add up."

Dirk nodded.

"I think she is siphoning off money from dormant accounts," Sanya said, "maybe in small increments."

"There is no evidence of that," Dirk said.

"Then maybe you should look closer at her new friend Stephen with the yacht; they are way too chummy for employer and employee," Sanya suggested, "maybe they are in it together."

"Good suggestion," Dirk nodded, "I am already on that. It was one of the reasons why I left early."

"And when you get Alex, is she going to jail? Will there be a perp walk? I want to see her arrested and in cuffs."

Dirk chuckled. "I don't know. When I find evidence of fraud, I hand it over to the shareholders. They will decide whether or not to give it to the police or handle it internally. One thing's for sure, she will have to pay back all the money she has spent so far."

"Good," Sanya said, "but I want her in jail for calling me a money-grubber and a penny pincher."

Dirk laughed. "Last I checked, penny-pinching was not really an insult. It just means you are careful with your coins."

"Well, money grubber then," Sanya said, "I am not someone who has money as my main interest and will do anything to get it. That's her. She was projecting."

"Was she always like this?" Dirk asked, "I've been trying to build a personality profile on her."

"No, actually," Sanya said, "I guess the money she's stealing got to her head. In high school, she was great. She and Cayenne are closer, but I didn't mind. We hung out, laughed, chatted, and shared our joys and sorrows. You know, the usual."

Dirk nodded.

"And then we graduated, some of us didn't go to college or went part-time, like Cayenne and Jerome. But we kept in touch, went places as a group, and had fun. Alex added a couple of friends along the way, and when we stayed at a guest house, our bills got smaller, so we were happy for that."

"Alex and Cayenne are similar in personality; they are happy, upbeat girls. They are pretty, look good in anything, and have a sweet disposition. I will miss Alex as a friend if I am going, to be honest. I was sick once, and she came to stay with me; my parents weren't home. I couldn't get up or do anything for myself. She didn't have to do it and there was nothing in it for her."

"That's admirable," Dirk said.

"And last year, when my car was out of commission for two weeks, Alex lent me her car."

"Now that's friendship," Dirk said.

"But I'll still have Cayenne," Sanya mused. "Cayenne is the friend who never forgets your birthday and is willing to celebrate however you want. She always calls you up when you need to talk. I can tell her anything, and she listens to me. She is an empathetic listener."

"Whenever I feel down or overwhelmed, Cayenne is the one who shows up with a comforting smile and a warm hug, armed with my favorite snacks and a playlist of songs she knows I love. She can sense when something is wrong, even if I haven't said a word. It's like she's tuned into my emotions on a frequency only she can hear.

"Cayenne's loyalty is unwavering; she stands by me through thick and thin. Do you know how hard it is to have good female friendships in this day and age? It can be as hard as finding a guy; trust me when I tell you."

Dirk grinned. "I believe you."

"So what about girlfriends? You have any?" Sanya asked.

"Not at the moment, no," Dirk said. "I was in a relationship, and it ended when she got a job offer in a different state. No hard feelings on either side."

"Oh," Sanya nodded. "What about you?" Dirk asked.

"I have a three-year on-and-off situation with someone," Sanya made a face, "Currently, we are not on, and we're not off; the bar is in the middle, just hanging there."

Dirk laughed. "Why?"

"Because he is studying medicine," Sanya shrugged, "and too busy for me, we agreed not to bother each other about spending time together. The pressure is off. We talk when we can. But he did send me chocolate for Valentine's Day and a huge bouquet of flowers at my workplace. And we did have dinner…"

Dirk smiled. "What can you tell me about Cayenne's past boyfriends?"

Sanya laughed. "Cayenne has dated several men; people are drawn to her personality and always ask her out. But as it relates to anything serious, I don't know of anyone. I think that Lance's guy messed things up for her. She's always trying to recreate her feelings with him and falling short."

Dirk couldn't help the smile that crossed his face.

Sanya looked at him suspiciously. "You are him, aren't you?"

"Now, why would you say that?" Dirk asked mildly.

"Just a hunch," Sanya shrugged. "I suggested it to Cayenne

already, and she dismissed it."

"See," Dirk said. "She dismissed it."

Sanya snorted. "She is not used to trusting her instincts, but I am. And I say you are Lance and you liked her too from back then. When you are ready to come clean, let me know the backstory. Until then, I won't say anything to Cayenne."

"You would make one hell of a detective," Dirk murmured.

Chapter Thirteen

"Hey, Cayenne, wake up," Sanya said.

Cayenne cracked an eye open and then another.

"You slept like a baby," Sanya beamed at her, "but we are at your house now. I called your sister, Sage; I can't believe she has the same number. I asked her to let us in. I had to tell her that you had an argument with Alex, and that's why you are home a day earlier than planned."

Cayenne groaned; her brain was fuzzy. What had happened? Where was she?

"And Sage said she would be at home," Sanya was still talking, "otherwise, I would have stayed with you. I don't want you to be alone at this time. Obviously, what Alex said was a shocker."

"Oh my god," Cayenne sat up and held her head, "I am a eunuch."

And then she looked across at Dirk.

He smiled at her. Was that pity in his smile?

"Hey," he said.

"Hey," Cayenne leaned back in the car seat; she probably looked a puffy-eyed mess. But what did it matter? She was a eunuch. She might as well never look pretty again.

She rubbed her temples. "Thanks for the lift home."

She tried not to maintain eye contact with Dirk. "It was nice to meet you, Dirk."

"Likewise," he said. "I'll call you tomorrow and check up on you."

She nodded; he was just being polite. They were parked right outside her townhouse. The door was opened and Sage was standing there.

"Girlfriend," Sanya kissed her on the cheek. "We will do our usual Sunday chats. At least you can sleep in the comfort of your bed tonight with your AC blasting cold."

Cayenne smiled wanly. "You are a good friend, Sanya."

Sanya nodded and stepped back.

They watched her as she went inside, then drove away. Cayenne slid all the way down the door.

Sage looked at her curiously. "What's wrong?"

"I had an argument with Alex. Well, not really an argument. Alex was jealous that Dirk seemed to like me."

"Dirk is the guy you're interested in?" Sage asked.

"Yup," Cayenne nodded.

"Ooh," Sage grinned.

"We hung out together a bit today on Stephen's yacht; we danced and laughed, but it was only for a little while. I was in a funk; he was helping me out of it."

"Why were you in a funk?" Sage asked, "You are never in a funk."

"Well, Stephen is our cousin; he is to call our father uncle."

"What? Alex's boss?"

"Yes," Cayenne inhaled. "Apparently, our father has

been a regular child abuser for years. He even abused his nieces, Stephen's sisters, and little girls in the community. He was protected by his parents and even his sister when he molested her girls. And that's not all; he will be released any day now."

"But he is supposed to be in jail for twenty years!" Sage said. "This would be a year early!"

"I know," Cayenne said, "Stephen said, according to his psychiatrist and spiritual advisers, he is reformed." Cayenne sighed. "Sadly, I don't think he can help himself. I would never in a million years be comfortable with him around children."

Sage nodded. "I wonder if Mom will try to kill him again?"

Cayenne closed her eyes. "Maybe, I don't know. Maybe she is long past that. What I want to know from her is why she didn't tell me that I was abused so badly I had to have reconstructive surgery on my privates, and I don't have any ovaries."

"Say what now?" Sage widened her eyes.

"Court papers, Alex, in her burning desire to taint me before Dirk, blurted out that she read in our father's court documents that I had been molested so bad my insides were rearranged and reconstructed. And that I was not really a woman at all. In fact, I am a eunuch. And my personal pronouns should be they/them."

Sage chuckled. "You laughed at her, right?"

"No," Cayenne said, "I don't know if it's true."

"How could you not know if it's true?" Sage frowned, "You get your periods, right?"

"Yes," Cayenne nodded, "but I didn't get one until I was seventeen."

"Doesn't matter," Sage said, "menstruating means you have ovaries. Ovaries mean you are not a female eunuch."

"What about the reconstruction bit?" Cayenne asked, "Was I raped so badly I had to be stitched up and reconstructed?"

"That I don't know. How does down there look?"

"Like a regular vagina," Cayenne said. "I never thought about it before; it was just there. Doesn't all of them look basically the same?"

Sage laughed. "You are fine, Cayenne. I can't believe that you know your own body, and you had Alex telling people that you are not really a woman."

"But she had a point," Cayenne said, "nobody has aroused me since Lance. I barely get a shift on the feelings scale for anyone else in six years. That's not normal. Maybe I am really damaged, my nerve endings or something. I am going to have to do some research about it."

"So what about Alex's guy, the one you spent time with? How did he make you feel?"

"Like Lance did," Cayenne got up, "he looks the same, talks the same, they could be twins. And I feel the same way I did. Surely, I can be forgiven for getting my wires crossed."

"Mmm," Sage nodded, "a Lance look-alike was the only one to get your parts humming, and now he hears that you have reconstructed parts."

"I know, right," Cayenne flung herself on the settee. "I am not going to see him again. After hearing about my so-called impediments, he will ghost me. And as for Alex, we may never talk again."

"What she said to you was pretty low," Sage sat across from Cayenne. "And what is she doing reading court circulars about Paul Aubry's case? That's weird."

"I know, right," Cayenne said, "why haven't I thought to read them?"

"Because it's awful stuff," Sage said, "and it's about what

our father did to you."

Cayenne grimaced. "Mom always said she caught him before he could go further. So why am I in the court records as being dinged up to the point of surgery?"

"Ask Mom," Sage said.

"I will not get a straight answer," Cayenne sighed. She won't be pleased to hear that Paul will be released soon; that will consume her. She'll deflect and talk me in circles. I know my mother. She didn't want me to know because she didn't want me to worry. But despite all of that, I will make an attempt to get an answer from her. I'll visit her at work."

"Good idea," Sage nodded. "If she is at work, then it means she is on medication and relatively stable."

Cayenne chuckled. "Mom would take offense at you saying that."

"It's the truth," Sage slunk back into the settee. Do you want something to eat, or are you full from the yacht party?"

"Full," Cayenne said, "thanks for asking." She laid down fully on the settee. "I don't have the energy to go upstairs. By the way, what are you doing here? I thought you were spending the weekend at Brian's grandparents' house."

"I was," Sage nodded, "but I changed my mind; his father will be there."

"So?" Cayenne frowned.

"So I have a terrible, awful, monstrous crush on him," Sage said. "I need it to subside before I face him again."

"You have a crush on Mr. Whitlock?" Cayenne asked.

"I do," Sage replied, putting her head in her hands. "I can't shake it. I wish I hadn't told Brian to give him my resume. I'll have to work with him every day. Uh, I won't be able to hide my feelings."

"What's a landscaping company doing with a social media manager?" Cayenne asked sleepily.

Sage sighed, her face still buried in her hands. "They're trying to expand their online presence, showcase their work, and attract more clients. You know, the usual stuff businesses do nowadays."

Cayenne nodded slowly, her eyelids growing heavier. "I guess that makes sense. But it's just so...unexpected."

Sage chuckled softly. "Tell me about it. I never thought I'd be interested in landscaping content, but here we are. I spend too much time looking at landscape makeover shows. And I would love the opportunity to see it close up."

"Tell me about Mr. Whitlock. Is he cute like Brian?"

"Yup, but he is far better looking. Brian resembles his mom, not his dad." Sage said dreamily, "Bruce Whitlock is smart and charming, and there's something about him that just draws me in."

Cayenne's eyes fluttered closed. "How smart could he be? Wasn't Brian born when he was in high school?"

"No, Sage said, "he was eighteen and just entering college. People make mistakes, Cayenne. We are not going to bash him for his. He was a teenage father, but that didn't mean he was some roving playboy. Brian is his only child to date, and he has since become a success!"

"Okay," Cayenne murmured. "No need to defend your man crush."

Sage sighed. "I have been feeling this way since I met him. I need help! I can't even tell Brian this. How do you say to your boyfriend, I have a serious crush on your dad?"

"Sounds complicated. But maybe it's just a phase. Crushes can be like that. Remember my six-year crush on Lance?"

Sage nodded thoughtfully. "Why are you talking about it like it's in the past? When you left here, you were still pro-Lance."

"But now I am pro-Dirk," Cayenne murmured sleepily.

"But it won't do me any good. I am sure I won't see or hear from him again. Maybe when the next Lance look-alike comes to town, we'll have a seamless, drama-free romance on our way to our happily ever after."

Chapter Fourteen

Dirk stared at his phone, the contact list glowing softly in the dim light of the pool house.   His thumb hovered over Cayenne's name.

He had gotten her number from Sanya and had memorized it already. Should he call, or shouldn't he?

Maybe he shouldn't, not yet. Let her sleep it off. It had been an exhausting day.

He was not exhausted, though he was energized. He was about to solve this case.

He knew exactly what he was looking for now. It had to be an account that was given to Alex six months ago. It also had something to do with Cayenne.

After Stephen saw Alex in the parking lot with Cayenne, two things had happened. Alex had gotten a promotion and had access to more substantial accounts, and her spending spree had started.

Dirk went for his laptop.

If his theory was correct, one of the accounts she was working on was being tampered with. But somehow, it was bypassing the auditors' scrutiny.

An idea was forming in his head. Cayenne said a lawyer called her mother and told her that Paul Aubry had set up an investment account for his girls. Anise had basically told the man to kick rocks and that she didn't want anything to do with her ex.

But that did not negate the fact that the account was there. He was almost certain LAD Wealth had managed it for the past twenty years. By now, its net asset value would be astronomical.

He needed to know the name of that account and who could withdraw from it. He had a sneaking suspicion that he was dealing with fraud, forgery, and embezzlement.

Dirk's fingers flew over the keyboard as he logged into the company's secure database. First, he accessed the list of accounts under Alex's management. There were dozens, but he was only interested in the ones that had shown unusual activity over the past six months.

He filtered the data, searching for accounts with significant withdrawals or transfers coinciding with Alex's spending spree.

One account stood out: an investment portfolio under the name: "Rodin Holdings." It had several sub-accounts attached to it. One sub-account, in particular, had seen substantial activity recently, including large sums being transferred to various obscure entities.

It could be totally legitimate. He wouldn't jump to conclusions but needed to know who controlled Rodin Holdings.

The company details would be on file. He searched for them. Matthew Beckett, an attorney at law, was the principal of that company. Dirk took down Matthew Beckett's contact details. He would call him first thing on Tuesday. It was a holiday and a long weekend, but he felt as if this information had some teeth in it.

This was where an auditor would stop the search. There was nothing to see here. Everything seemed to be in order. Withdrawals, especially in large sums, could only be authorized by two senior personnel at LAD. He searched for the two signatures, Alexandria Hall and Stephen Grant.

That in itself was not significant. Stephen supervised many of Alex's accounts.

Before he closed the computer, he searched for Rodin. The first name that came up on his search list was Francois Auguste Rene Rodin, generally considered the founder of modern sculpting and the creator of the famous piece, the Thinker.

Jackpot! Wasn't Paul Aubry a sculptor of some repute?

He went down the rabbit hole of research once more and he came up with an article about the man.

Paul Aubry is a sculptor known for his intricate and thought-provoking pieces. His works have been displayed in galleries worldwide, earning him a significant reputation in the art community. Paul Aubry's sculptures often explore themes of human emotion and existential contemplation, drawing parallels to Rodin's famous works.

Dirk scrolled through several articles and images of Paul Aubry's sculptures, admiring the craftsmanship and depth of each piece. Unsurprisingly his works were usually of children or young women.

He found a detailed biography of Paul Aubry on an art history website. The biography mentioned that Paul had two daughters, Cayenne and Sage and that his work often reflected his turbulent personal life. There was no mention that he was currently incarcerated for child molestation.

It was highly likely that a man who patterned himself off Rodin would name his company Rodin. It was logical; it didn't have to be true, though. He would confirm soon.

Paul's lawyer, Matthew Beckett, was probably his proxy. He closed the laptop and rubbed the back of his neck. He needed more facts. However, he would have to wait for Tuesday to find out what was going on. Tomorrow was free. And he wasn't thinking of spending it with anybody else but Cayenne.

On a whim, he texted her, Are you up to hanging out tomorrow?

He didn't expect to hear from her; she was probably sleeping.

He was getting up and heading for the bedroom when she texted, Sure, where and when.

He racked his brain, thinking about something to do that wasn't too far or too strenuous but would be fun. They both liked photography; he hadn't picked up a camera in ages, and Irish Town was a nice low-key place to visit and take loads of pictures in the serene scenery of the Jamaican Blue Mountains. They could hike, explore the area, and capture some beautiful shots together.

How about a trip to Irish Town? We could hike to my favorite cafe and take photos, renew our photography hobby. Meet at 9 AM? he suggested.

That sounds amazing! See you then, she replied almost immediately. I'll have to go charge my camera.

He sent her a smiley face emoji and went to lie down.

This weekend had not ended the way he had thought it would. But was he sad about it? No. He was happy he was seeing Cayenne again.

This may be the right time for them. She still had feelings

for him, and after a day and a night, he found that he wasn't immune to her either, not by a long shot.

Chapter Fifteen

At nine, Dirk pulled up in front of Cayenne's apartment. She was already waiting outside, her face lighting up when she saw him. She climbed into the passenger seat, and he smiled at her.

"So we meet again, Miss Aubry."

Cayenne nodded. "I doubted that I would see you again after what Alex said. I was literally shocked last night, then I squealed. It earned me a kick from my sister."

Dirk laughed. "Which sister?"

"Sage." Cayenne smiled. "My other sister, Cinnamon, doesn't live with us anymore. She is married to Jaxon Wilde and living in the hills."

"I see," Dirk nodded.

"So why do you want to see me again?" Cayenne turned to him.

"I feel the beginnings of an emotional attachment," Dirk said. "I think you are fun. I want to get to know you better;

I find you intriguing. I could go on."

"Please do," Cayenne grinned.

"I like your smile, your sense of humor, and I am not intimidated by your, ah... condition."

Cayenne frowned. "I don't think I have a condition. I know I am normal. I double-checked to be sure."

Dirk looked at her and smiled. "What did checking involve?"

"Three mirrors and a high-powered flashlight," Cayenne nodded. "If I am reconstructed or whatever it is, it was good work. And for your information, I do get aroused. I felt it with Lance and now..."

"Me?" Dirk tightened his hand on the steering wheel.

"Uh-huh," Cayenne nodded.

"Good. Great," Dirk said in relief. "I like that Lance and I are the only ones who have gotten that response."

"That's not to say I am going to act on my feelings for you," Cayenne said. "I am quite particular and not easy."

"I am the same," Dirk smiled. "What's that famous Bob Marley quote, 'If she's amazing, she won't be easy.'"

Cayenne smiled. "And if she's worth it, you won't give up, and if you give up, you're not worthy."

"So now that we have that out of the way," Dirk said, "I wonder where the court got the information from."

"I have no clue," Cayenne sighed. "I called my mother last night after my thorough self-examination, and she said she couldn't talk to me unless it's an emergency. She was at a charity program. She supports a charity for victims of child sex abuse. She is passionate about it."

"Because of your abuse?" Dirk asked.

"No," Cayenne sighed. "Hers."

"Ah," Dirk sighed. "I hate abuse in general; to hear about child sex abuse is even more heart-wrenching."

"I know," Cayenne said. "That's why I haven't read my father's court file. I didn't want any memories being jogged because I honestly can't remember a thing, and it's just sad all around."

"I know what you mean," Dirk nodded.

"I think I should read it, though," Cayenne said. "It is public record. I can't keep pushing my head in the sand and then breaking down in tears like I did yesterday when someone reads it and assumes things about me. So I made up my mind. I am going to read it and then I am going to ask my mom about it. What Alex said and what my mother has told me about that time are two completely different stories."

"I'd offer to read it with you." Dirk said. "But I fear I would get really angry. I really can't handle certain injustices. Your father should have been castrated from a young age. But then again you wouldn't have been born. So there is that."

Cayenne sighed. "My father had a long history of pedophilia. Stephen said the family knew about it and shielded him from way back in the days. You are right, if he had been castrated then, I wouldn't have been here now."

Dirk drove up a particularly steep mountain and had to concentrate on the road that looked like it was made for single traffic. Cayenne took out her camera. "The view from this side of the road is awesome."

"I know," Dirk murmured. "Tell me about Stephen. What kind of relationship did he have with your dad?"

"I only know what he told me," Cayenne said. "He adored his uncle, and then the relationship was severed because of my dad's proclivities. He abused his nieces, Stephen's sisters, so they were forbidden to visit him."

"Sounds as if Paul Aubry can't help himself," Dirk murmured. "Are they absolutely sure that they want to let him out of jail? He will be sixty-five when he gets out. He won't be in his dotage."

"Ironically, I don't think Stephen was bothered by that." Cayenne frowned. "He sounded bitter that my father inherited everything, and the rest of the family got hardly a penny to rub together. I don't know why he was so upset about that; he is obviously a man who can afford his own things."

"How did the Aubry family make their money?" Dirk asked.

"They had old money from generations ago. They have land, manufacturing, tin mining—you name it, they were in it, or so I heard," Cayenne turned the camera to him. "Smile."

Dirk smiled.

Cayenne lowered the camera. "I wish I had photos of Lance. I could show you one and shock you with it."

"If we date, am I always going to be in Lance's shadow?" Dirk stopped at the sign that said 'To Hiking Trail and Cafe.' The place was lush and green around them. He turned to Cayenne. "So, am I going to be in his shadow?"

"Maybe," Cayenne smiled. "If you had some distinguishing features apart from him, and if you didn't make me feel the same way, I'd stop the comparisons. But you don't, so are you jealous?"

"Not really," Dirk said. "What you and I will have will be deep and real. Not a friends-only situation. Do you think you can handle that?"

"Of course I can," Cayenne said. "I am twenty-three, I have dated before, many, many times. I just have not gone further than kisses with these guys. I can't turn my brain off during a kiss. I am usually thinking about hair or grocery lists. It's nothing like they write about in romance books. I am not lost in the moment or caught up in a conflagration of flames or—"

Dirk leaned forward and placed his lips on hers while she was mid-talk.

For a moment, Cayenne's eyes widened in surprise, but then she closed them, leaning into the kiss. It wasn't hurried or intense, but gentle and searching. As Dirk pulled back, he studied her face, a smile playing on his lips.

Cayenne took a deep breath, her hand touching her lips softly. "That was... different."

"Different good or different bad?" Dirk asked, his tone teasing yet sincere.

"Different good," she replied, a small smile creeping onto her face. "I didn't think about anything else. This is how I imagined it would be with Lance. You see, we never kissed. He was such a perfect gentleman."

Dirk smiled. "Cayenne, do me a favor."

"What?" Cayenne whispered.

"Take Lance off the pedestal you had him on. He doesn't deserve it. He is a man. He showed some restraint around you, listened to your conversation, and in general, he presented himself as non-threatening. Maybe because he knew about your past, and he wanted you to have a positive relationship with a male figure who was undemanding sexually and yet friendly.

"But trust me when I tell you this: he had moments where he wouldn't have minded stripping you of your clothes, kissing you all over, and taking you on his couch. He was a male with all that entails. He just had self-control. Don't deify him."

Cayenne gasped.

"Come on," Dirk said, "we have loads of pictures to take, and I am really looking forward to drinking Blue Mountain coffee in the Blue Mountains."

****

They hiked to the café in the hills, taking lovely pictures along the way. The café was perfectly located, with a patio overlooking the lush greenery of the Blue Mountains. They sat there, eating freshly baked pastries and sipping steaming cups of locally brewed coffee. The air was crisp and invigorating, filled with the scent of pine and the distant sound of birdsong.

Cayenne leaned back in her chair, a contented sigh escaping her lips. "This place is incredible. I can't believe I've never been here before."

Dirk smiled, pleased with her reaction. "It's one of my favorite spots. My parents had us coming up here every Sunday when I was younger. It was our family time. I thought I'd share it with you."

"Thank you, I appreciate it. I needed some time to clear my mind."

"Have you heard from Alex yet?" Dirk asked.

"She sent me like a thousand texts," Cayenne shrugged. "I am not responding yet. I am going to let her simmer. She needs to explain to me why she was hiding the things she knew about me and then just throw it in my face like that. She was willing to throw away ten years of friendship over a guy."

"Maybe it goes deeper than that," Dirk said. "Alex and I had no relationship whatsoever. I would see her at work, we'd say hi. I accepted her invitation for the weekend after she told me there would be twelve other people there. It wasn't supposed to be misconstrued as a romantic interlude whatsoever. You are missing something."

"I may be," Cayenne sighed. "I am going to give her at least a week before I pick this up again. In the meantime, I don't want to talk about her."

"Good," Dirk said. "Tell me more about you. What makes Cayenne tick?"

"What makes me tick?" Cayenne took a moment to consider the question, tracing the rim of her coffee cup with her finger. "I guess I'm still figuring that out. I love my work, I love my family and friends, including she who we are not going to talk about. I love volunteering. I am a member of several charities, I have a full life but sometimes, lately, I catch myself wanting to have a true romance, walking in the rain holding hands, and feeling that electric connection with someone who truly understands me."

She sighed, a wistful smile playing on her lips. "It's not like I need someone to complete me or anything. I just... I want to share all these moments with someone who gets it, you know? Who gets me."

Dirk nodded thoughtfully, leaning back in his chair. "That makes sense. It's natural to want companionship, especially when you have so much to give."

Cayenne looked at him searchingly, "What about you, Dirk? What makes you tick?"

He chuckled softly, rubbing the back of his neck. "Well, I'm a simple guy, really. I love my job, though it can be demanding. I love my family, I'm always up for an adventure, whether it's hiking in the mountains or trying out a new recipe. But, like you, I've been feeling that tug lately. The desire for something deeper, more meaningful. I guess we have a lot in common."

She nodded. "It's funny, I never thought that I would feel like this about anyone again. "

"Cayenne," Dirk's gaze held hers. "I have something to

tell you…"

Her phone rang, breaking the spell. She answered it without looking at the call display. "Hello?"

"Cayenne, it's Marg. Can you do a house call for me tomorrow? I know it's a holiday, but I made the arrangement a couple of months ago, and other than me, you are the best braider I know."

Cayenne chuckled. "Why can't you make it?"

"I sprained my ankle and broke two fingers today. Needless to say, I won't be coming into the shop for a couple of weeks. I already asked Netta to reassign my clients."

"Oh wow," Cayenne murmured. "Sorry to hear. Yes, I'll fill in for you."

"I'll text over the name of the client and the address. It's a house call, and it's for her youngest daughter. She is going to do a dance recital the same day, so you'll have to go early."

"Okay," Cayenne said.

She hung up the phone and looked at Dirk. "I am going to do a house call tomorrow, filling in for a coworker."

"We'll hang out the day after," Dirk smiled. "Unfortunately, tomorrow I have some work to do that I have been neglecting for an overseas client."

"What was it that you were going to tell me?" Cayenne asked.

"It can wait," Dirk said.

Chapter Sixteen

Sage wasn't in when she got back from her date. Cayenne pottered around the house, got her supplies together for her job in the morning, and called the client to ensure the appointment was still on.

She was pleasantly tired; she would take an early night, but first, she texted Dirk to ensure he got home safely.

He was home.

And then she realized that she didn't know where home was.

My parents' pool house for now. He texted back. New York, usually.

That caused a little shock. She thought he lived here in Jamaica. She said as much.

Dirk texted back, I'll tell you more by the end of the week.

Cayenne thought she was going to think about that for the whole night, but she had some reading to do, the child sex abuse case involving Paul Aubry. In it, she was referred to as a minor child. Some of the details were not available because of the graphic nature of the acts, but she read enough to be troubled.

Why didn't she remember any of that?

She saw why Alex thought she was a female eunuch. The doctor in the case said she was severely damaged. She wasn't.

She closed her eyes and drifted to sleep, only waking up when her sister closed the door to her room.

"Never ever date a guy and then fall in love with his father," Sage said dramatically when Cayenne met her on the landing on her way to the bathroom.

Cayenne was too groggy to follow up with Sage's issues right now.

"Can we talk about this in the morning?" she asked.

"Oh no," Sage said. "This is not going to be spoken about again. I am going to bury my feelings for Bruce Whitlock deeply, very deeply. And I will never take them out or examine them again."

Cayenne groaned and returned to bed, only waking up when her alarm shrieked. She had made plans to be at the Morgans' place by nine.

****

Morgan's mansion in the hills was close to where her sister lived. She would pop over and visit after she was done. She missed her nephew. Cinnamon would be surprised to see her this weekend.

Sanya texted her when she was driving up to the house. Anton said Alex had been so grumpy since we left that they kept out of her way. The weekend was a washout after that.

Cayenne smiled. Good. She texted back. Call you later.

Filling in for a coworker.

She hung up the phone, got out of the car, and admired the house and the gardens for a little bit. It was one of those split-level houses that looked deceptively like a single-story house at the front but had more stories at the back. It was built to take advantage of the views of the surrounding hills.

"Oh, hello, Cayenne," a tall, elegant lady greeted her. She had striking high cheekbones, almond-shaped eyes, full pillow lips, and wore her hair in a curly pixie cut. She bore a striking resemblance to a model she had just seen at the side of a city bus selling insurance. "I think I just saw you on the side of a city bus," Cayenne said.

She laughed. "Yes, that's me, my husband's insurance company. They roped me into doing the ad, and now I am famous. My name is Heather Morgan. My daughter, Emily, needs the braids. If you could come this way, our basement is part hairdressing parlor, part movie theater, and games room; Marg helped me design the hairdressing side."

Cayenne smiled.

"I was so sorry to hear about Marg. She has been styling Emily for all her recitals, and she knows what is required, but she reassures me that you are great with children and that I shouldn't worry."

"I'll try my best to make this as smooth an operation as possible," Cayenne said as they descended the stairs to the first floor. She had expected it to be dark, but the area was surrounded by glass doors that opened up to a patio and neatly manicured gardens. Beyond that, she could see a pool and then a pool house. It was a view worthy of a hotel.

Inside the open-concept space was a bar area with stools, a lounge area with a giant television screen, and several plush couches arranged around it for comfort while watching the screen. The décor was modern yet cozy. Its walls were adorned with tasteful photographic pieces depicting different nature scenes.

Heather led her to an area that mimicked a station in a hairdressing parlor. Everything was there, including a large mirror with flattering lighting, a sleek, adjustable salon chair, and an array of professional-grade hair products neatly organized on a counter. Various brushes, combs, and styling tools, including high-end hairdryers and curling irons, were all within easy reach. The setup was complete with a washbasin for rinsing and shampooing hair, making it a fully functional mini-salon.

"Wow, it's nice down here," Cayenne said.

Heather smiled. "Thank you. I don't like going to the salon and waiting for hours, even with an appointment. I found that I usually had to wait, so I designed my own salon and have my hairdresser do house calls."

Cayenne nodded. "It makes sense if you have the means."

Emily came down the stairs. She was a poised little girl who really glided like a ballerina. She was a darker-skinned version of her mother, with a cloud of hair almost reaching her waist.

"Am I braiding her hair or using extensions?" Cayenne asked.

"Braiding her hair," Heather said.

"Oh," Cayenne nodded, "it makes sense seeing the length. I totally misunderstood."

"No problem," Heather said. "Please braid the hair with an updo in mind; she has to compete later today."

"Okay," Cayenne nodded.

"And these are her products," Heather pointed to the hair butter and gel normally used.

Cayenne paused. Besides the products, there was a magazine, Diaspora Magazine, on the front page was a smiling picture of Dirk James.

"Wait a minute," she whispered, "I know him."

"You do?" Heather smiled. "How nice. Dirk is my son, my firstborn, the first of five."

"Is that so?" Cayenne whispered. She looked at the magazine's topic, 'Black Men Under Thirty Making Waves.'

"What is he making waves about?" Cayenne cleared her throat.

"Oh, he is a forensic accountant," Heather said, settling into the chair across from her. "If you read the article, you'll see he has solved many financial fraud cases. I am quite proud of him."

Cayenne nodded. "So, er, what is he doing in Jamaica?"

"A favor for his stepfather," Heather said. "If you want that magazine, I have loads more. I may have contributed to it being their best-selling issue."

Cayenne chuckled. "I'll take it."

"So, where do you know him from?" Heather asked.

"Well, I, er, we stayed at the same place this weekend," Cayenne said, "he resembled a friend of mine, Lance Cauldwell, and I kind of…"

Heather started laughing.

"What's so funny?" Cayenne asked, bewildered.

"Well, he is Lance Cauldwell," Heather said. "I initially gave him my maiden name when he was born. He changed it to his father's surname six years ago. His father's first name was Lancelot, and I gave it to Dirk as a middle name. When he migrated and started working with his paternal grandparents, he stopped going by the name Lance at their request, painful memories and all of that."

"Oh," Cayenne murmured. She parted Emily's hair and started plaiting it.

"Dirk and I are going for ice cream after my competition,"

Emily said. "He said we could both do with a break."

"Is that so?" Cayenne said.

"Oh yes," Emily nodded.

"No nodding, dear," Heather said gently.

"So how is it that you were friends with Lance and didn't know of his name change?" Heather asked.

"I think it has something to do with the case he is working on," Cayenne said grimly. "He pretended not to be Lance or even to know me because the person he is investigating for fraud is my best friend."

"Oh my," Heather said, "oh my. Did I give it away? Am I at fault? I don't want to jeopardize his investigation. He has been at this now for two months."

"I don't want to jeopardize things either," Cayenne said. "He is right not to have told me earlier. I may have said something to my friend, but now I'll try to pretend that I don't know a thing."

Chapter Seventeen

It took Cayenne four hours to do Emily Morgan's hair. It was a little after one o'clock when she finished. She had refused to stay for lunch with Heather and her family. She had been on tenterhooks as it was, waiting for Dirk to find her doing his sister's hair. It had still not sunk in that Dirk was Lance, and Lance was Dirk.

She had been right all along.

She chuckled a little as she drove toward her sister's house. As she told Heather earlier, she understood why he couldn't have been straight with her initially, but she still felt weird about all those things she had said about Lance. He knew she was talking about him, and he kept a straight face.

Goodness, he knew how she felt about him. How did it make him feel hearing her declare her love for him and calling him perfect?

He had said he didn't want to be put on a pedestal.

Fair enough.

But he liked her too; he had kissed her yesterday. He had asked her to go out with him while thinking that she was probably a mutilated woman with no sexual organs. That had to count for something, right?

She drove up to Cinnamon and Jax's house. They had the same unfettered view of the city as the Morgans.

Her mother's car was in the driveway. That was serendipitous; she could ask her why she was represented in the court files as being severely abused.

Anise usually visited Cinnamon's place on a whim to visit her grandson, VJ. VJ was a sweet little thing, and the first-time grandmother was obsessed with him.

She would be mellow. Maybe this would be her window to ask and receive satisfactory responses. One could only hope, Cayenne thought darkly; one never knew what Anise would divulge from her closet of secrets.

Cinnamon greeted her at the door after she knocked. "Sister!"

"Sister!" They hugged.

"You smell so good," Cayenne said. "What's that perfume?"

"My mother-in-law's latest, it's called Intoxicated," Cinnamon said.

"I want it," Cayenne said seriously. "It's amazing."

"Come keep me company," Cinnamon said. "I am in the kitchen finishing up dinner. Jax and Mom are on the patio with VJ; you can tell me everything that is happening with you."

"Oh, mom is your only visitor?" Cayenne asked.

"Yes," Cinnamon glanced at her, "why?"

"I wanted to quiz her about something," Cayenne said. "I might as well tell you before so you are up to date."

She sat at the breakfast nook and regaled her sister with the latest happenings.

"So, Lance is Dirk, and he is investigating Alex," Cinnamon remarked.

"That's right," Cayenne nodded.

"Don't tell her and obstruct his investigation," Cinnamon warned.

"I won't," Cayenne said.

"I am not convinced," Cinnamon looked at her. "You and Alex are as tight as thieves."

"Not anymore," Cayenne said. "You should have seen how she came at me a day ago. I think we are done."

"How often have you two quarreled, and you say you are done?" Cinnamon asked.

"Many," Cayenne said.

"And then you hug it out," Cinnamon said. "If she is stealing, Cayenne, she needs to be stopped. It's not right to take someone else's money."

"I know," Cayenne sighed.

"I knew I heard your voice," Anise said behind them. "My dearest Cayenne."

As usual, her mother greeted her in her over-the-top way.

Anise hugged her and then stepped back. "What's wrong? You look a little off."

"I wanted to talk to you about something," Cayenne said, "and I know how you get when serious matters are on the table."

"Hit me," Anise said. "I am doing much better these days. Ask anyone."

"Stephen Grant," Cayenne jumped right in, "I spent a day on his yacht two days ago. It was a party."

Anise frowned. "Stephen has a yacht? How can he afford a yacht?"

"I don't know," Cayenne said. "He is the managing director at LAD Wealth Management. He's Alex's boss. He told me about Paul and his family; I didn't know we were cousins."

"He is your cousin, yes," Anise said, "but nobody from that family is worth knowing, including your father. Stephen is not as terrible, but the man has an axe to grind with Paul, which spilled over on me."

"Because Paul is a child abuser?" Cayenne asked.

"No," Anise said, "because Paul inherited millions from his father as the firstborn. Your grandfather did not share the wealth equitably. Paul said to me once that his dad once told him that he had the same problems he did. At the time, I didn't know what the problem was. Now I know.

"Anyway," Anise said, "Stephen has always been in a funk over that. I told him to let it go years ago. He called me stupid for not accepting the trust fund your father set up for you and Sage. I told him I didn't want the dirty money. At the time, I was too angry to think straight."

"What trust fund?" Cinnamon asked curiously.

"He put a couple million in a trust for Cayenne and Sage. They could draw from it when they turned eighteen," Anise explained. "His lawyer told me about it, and I told him to stuff it. I was not interested. Looking back, I may have acted too rashly. It wasn't mine to deny. He did owe you girls for being the worst father on the planet. I should call the lawyer and find out how it's going. You and Sage should decide what to do with the money."

"Rightly so," Cinnamon nodded.

Cayenne sighed. "I don't know how to feel about that. As of now, I am indifferent. Did you know Paul is being released soon? Stephen said any day now."

"I didn't know about that," Anise said, "but I expect he'll soon be back in prison when he comes out and rapes another young child."

"Mom!" Cayenne said.

"He can't help himself," Anise said. "I did my part in putting him away, and it almost didn't happen. He knows who to pay off in law enforcement to keep things quiet. How do you think he got away with his actions for years? They enabled him by turning a blind eye. The parents of the children who didn't carry him to court, who accepted money to keep their mouths shut, the police who have seen with their own eyes the damage that man has wrought and take a payment instead.

"Why on earth are they releasing him to the unsuspecting population? He's a true menace to the most vulnerable in our society. He is going to ruin many more lives unless someone castrates him."

"I read the court records," Cayenne said. "They described me as being so destroyed that I had to have reconstructive surgery."

Cinnamon gasped. "What?"

"That wasn't you," Anise said. "The case was about to be thrown out. It almost didn't see the light of day. I went to Dr. Douglas and begged him to help me."

"Dr. Douglas is who again?" Cayenne asked.

"The doctor who attended to four children that Paul had molested. He reported the assaults to the police and realized that nothing came of it. Parents were silenced, and Paul still walked free. After reading my story in the news, he contacted me and commended me for doing something about Paul.

"When I told him that Paul was getting off scot-free once again, we hatched a plan. He decided to use a girl similar in age to you, Paul's former housekeeper's daughter, and present it to the court as yours."

"Oh my God," Cinnamon whispered. "How bad was it?"

"Real bad. She almost died," Anise sighed. "I couldn't hold my lunch after what Dr. Douglas told me happened; it was awful. I agreed to use her information because it was gruesome enough that I think no one with a conscience could excuse it, no matter how much money they were getting. And that's how we got Paul off the streets."

"Oh," Cayenne said.

"I am not sorry I did it," Anise said. "I don't know how some people can live with themselves after seeing these things happen to their children and accept money to shut up. No, not me, never."

"Do you think he's reformed?" Cayenne asked quietly, her voice barely above a whisper. "Stephen said his psychiatrist and spiritual advisor think he is."

Anise sighed deeply. "People can change, but it's hard to be certain with someone like Paul. All we can do is hope."

Cayenne leaned back in her chair. "Thank you for telling me the truth, Mom. I needed to know."

"Well, now you do," Anise got up. "I need some fresh air."

Chapter Eighteen

Cayenne was sitting in the break room the next day, checking her messages. It was a little after one, and although the shop was buzzing with activity, she found herself between customers, relishing the time to catch up on her messages.

Dirk had written twice, once yesterday, to let her know he was thinking of her but was caught up in a meeting for most of the day.

Then, this morning, he asked her to dinner.

She replied, Yes, but added, Over at my house. I'll get something from Bud and Sally's. I'll be very tired.

Apparently, he didn't know his cover was blown or that she had been to his parents' house, just a stone's throw across from the pool house he was staying.

Alex's name flashed across the screen, but she let it go to voicemail again. She didn't have the energy to deal with her right now. She didn't trust herself not to blurt out that she knew what was happening.

Deep down, she was concerned for her friend and what was she involved in? Would she go to jail? Alex couldn't handle jail. Her parents would be so disappointed and humiliated. Cayenne was majorly tempted to say something. What if she texted Alex and told her, They are coming to get you, run?

That wouldn't be right.

She snapped out of it when Tasha sat in front of her. "I have to tell you about my long weekend. It involved a stakeout, a car chase, and proof that my boyfriend is not cheating on me but is secretly working another job so that he can afford a wedding ring."

Cayenne put down her phone. "Wow, that sounds more exciting than my weekend, and that was pretty wild."

****

Dirk entered the LAD Wealth building, his head buzzing with what he had just learned. He had spent a good chunk of the morning with Matthew Beckett, Paul Aubry's lawyer.

The case was all but over; he knew exactly what happened and how it happened. The executive board, the risk management committee, and the internal audit committee were all briefed. His job at LAD Wealth was done. Stephen and Alex's fate was now to be determined by the powers that be.

They both could easily be charged for fraud and embezzlement for starters. Usually, financial companies, in a bid to not cause an alarm to the rest of the clients, would handle it internally.

Handling it could range from discreetly terminating their employment to negotiating a quiet settlement. In more severe cases, it might involve reporting them to the authorities, but this was often seen as a last resort. The priority was always to maintain client confidence and protect the company's reputation.

Dirk strode through the polished marble lobby, nodding to the receptionist, who flashed a practiced smile. He felt a mix of relief and unease. The relief of having uncovered the truth was tempered by the knowledge of the storm that was about to hit. Stephen was managing director of LAD Wealth; the fallout would be significant.

His steps echoed in the quiet halls as he went to his office.

The evidence was damning, and he had gotten it all from Matthew Beckett, who had been shocked that something like that could happen under his watch—he had bank statements, forged documents, and secret emails.

He knew the board would take swift action; there was no other choice. The integrity of LAD Wealth was at stake. As soon as he entered the office, the phone on his desk rang, jolting him from his thoughts. It was the head of the risk management committee.

"Dirk, we've convened an emergency meeting. We need you in the boardroom in thirty minutes."

"I'll be there," Dirk replied, hanging up.

"Knock, knock," Alex said, pushing her head through the door. She smiled uncertainly.

Dirk sighed. "Miss Hall."

"Wow, no need to be so formal," Alex giggled. "I came to apologize for how I acted a couple of days ago. I was jealous because I like you a lot."

Dirk indicated to the chair across from his desk. "Alex, have a seat."

She sat down. "Can we start over?"

"No," Dirk said. "I have a confession to make. I came here to work at LAD Wealth two months ago because the auditor knew something was wrong but couldn't pinpoint it. Usually, when a situation like that happens, they call in a person like me. I am a forensic accountant."

"Oh," Alex's smile slid off her face.

"One of the first things I do when I enter a situation like this is to check the employees' spending habits. Are they suddenly rich? Can they afford things they couldn't because of a sudden surge in income? That kind of thing."

Alex swallowed.

"Needless to say, you came on my radar," Dirk leaned back in his chair. "That's why I was taking a keen interest in you and the accounts you manage."

"I am not stealing anything!" Alex got up. "I don't have to listen to this."

"But you do," Dirk said. "I accepted your invitation to stay at Sea Glass Villas because I wanted you to confess to me in your downtime. Your confession was a long shot, but I had to take it. And then I met Cayenne."

"Cayenne?" Alex sank back down in the seat.

"Your relationship with Cayenne was the key to the case," Dirk sighed. "A long time ago, I was pretty close to Cayenne. I had to pretend I wasn't Lance Cauldwell to throw her off my scent."

"You are Lance Cauldwell?" Alex asked, confused.

"I am Dirk Lance Cauldwell James," Dirk said.

"But… oh my," Alex murmured. "She was trying to tell me how much you looked like her major crush from back in the day, and I ignored her."

"If Cayenne knew what I was about," Dirk said, "I feared she would make you aware of my true intentions. I couldn't have that. I knew you were up to something, but I just couldn't pinpoint what. The party on Stephen's yacht solidified my suspicions. I knew that whatever was going on involved both of you. You were both up to something, his new yacht, your spending…"

"I am not up to anything," Alex said without heat. "I work and invest my money…"

"That's not true," Dirk said. "I have the evidence to submit to the risk management committee in a few minutes. I will recommend that your punishment be lighter than Stephen's. Only because you stumbled into a situation that was in the making years before you were born."

"What do you mean, years before I was born?" Alex asked, confused.

"When Stephen discovered that his uncle Paul Aubry inherited the bulk of the estate, he was bitter about it. His mother was never financially savvy, and she and her husband squandered her inheritance to the point where they became destitute.

"Paul Aubry may have been many things, but he wasn't a wastrel. He invested a chunk of the money he inherited from his father into LAD Wealth for himself and his daughters. He created a holding account named Rodin Holdings. Under the holding company, there were three accounts: one for him, one for his daughters Sage and Cayenne.

"Stephen plotted and schemed his way into a position here at this company to gain access to that money. He worked in finance, managing various banks, with LAD Wealth as his final goalpost. He knew the terms of the investment, maybe from a conversation with his uncle. Who knows?

"He knew that Cayenne and Sage could start withdrawing from their accounts as soon as they turned eighteen. But he didn't have any legitimate way to access any of the accounts, not with the checks and balances that LAD Wealth has in place. He would need the senior wealth manager who oversees the account and a VP or himself to authorize the withdrawals.

"That's where you came in. He needed a senior wealth manager to be in charge of the Rodin account, someone who could be easily manipulated to do his bidding. He knew you were Cayenne's friend and worked here, so you were the obvious pick.

"He bided his time until he saw Cayenne in the parking lot to give you the promotion and told you the story about Paul Aubry and how awful he was. He even suggested that you read the court files.

"And you read them, and you got angry. Then he told you not to tell Cayenne; she didn't want or need the money from her abusive father. How am I doing so far?"

Alex nodded. "It's as if you were there."

"Then, when you became a senior wealth manager, he practically handed you the Rodin account on a silver platter. Then he suggested that you contact Matthew Beckett from Cayenne's email and tell him you were ready to receive funds from the account. It wasn't hard for you to do. You two were so close that you actually sent the letter from her email address using her computer. I saw the letter you sent.

"Matthew, thinking he was dealing with Cayenne, didn't think twice about signing off on the withdrawals from the account because you copied her signature and then had Stephen as your witness. You were the middleman in all of this, Alex."

Alex looked down, avidly examining her fingernails. Tears streamed down her face.

"You are going to have to pay it all back," Dirk said.

"But I don't have that kind of money. Besides, I only got ten percent of it; Stephen took the rest," Alex said. "At least I ensured that Cayenne enjoyed as much of what I took while I had it. She didn't know or care about it anyway."

Dirk glanced at his watch. "I have a meeting shortly."

"Please don't tell anyone," Alex pleaded, her lips trembling. "I'll pay it back somehow. I'll sell my car… I'll…"

"Miss Hall," the HR Manager said from the door, "I've been trying to call your office. I am happy you haven't left the building. Could you please come with me to conference room two?"

Alex stood up, her eyes red-rimmed. "Help me, Dirk."

Dirk shook his head. This was the part of the job he didn't particularly like, but there was no avoiding it. "I'm sorry, Alex," he said quietly. "It's out of my hands now."

Alex followed the HR Manager out of the office, her shoulders slumped in defeat. Dirk watched her go, feeling sympathy but knowing he had done what was right.

He took a deep breath and prepared himself for the meeting ahead. He would have to go through all of this again, in even more detail, and then he would have to reveal all to Cayenne this evening.

Chapter Nineteen

Cayenne opened the door when Dirk knocked. "Oh, hey, Dirk, I just got in. I haven't even ordered the food yet."

"That's okay," Dirk said. "Today was a doozy. I have a confession to make and an explanation to give."

Before Cayenne could respond, Sage descended the stairs. "Lance, oh my goodness, what are you doing here?"

"I was working undercover at LAD Wealth, trying to crack a case," Dirk replied. "It's over now."

"So that means Alex is in jail?" Cayenne spun around to face him.

"Wait a minute," Dirk narrowed his eyes, "you knew it was me all along?"

Cayenne chuckled. "No, I went to your parents' house yesterday, did your sister's hair, and got a copy of Diaspora Magazine when I left."

Dirk laughed. "And here I was, thinking that I would have to gently break the news to you."

"No need," Cayenne said.

"I wish I could stay to hear this story," Sage said, glancing at her watch. "But I promised Brian I'd meet him at the theater. Update me when I get back. It's good to see you again, Lance—er, Dirk. Which do you prefer?"

"I've gotten used to Dirk," he said with a smile.

"Well, Dirk, it is." Sage hugged him quickly and walked out the door, leaving Cayenne looking at him helplessly.

"So, where were we?" Dirk asked.

"You were about to have a seat. And you tell me everything," Cayenne said. "Including what happens to Alex."

Dirk sat down. "Well, where do I begin?"

"From where you left me, I mean here six years ago," Cayenne sat across from him.

Dirk grimaced. "I didn't mean to slink away like a thief in the night. I wanted to give you a clear break from me. I went to New York; I worked in my grandfather's firm. I changed my name to my father's name.

"I hadn't totally forgotten you over the years. I always thought you would be happily in a relationship by now. And I didn't want to intrude."

"When I saw you this weekend, little did I know that you would have been key to solving this case, and to think, I came to Jamaica two months ago to work on the case. If I hadn't gone for the weekend, I wouldn't have worked out the scheme that Alex and Stephen had cooking quite so readily; you were the key."

"What did they have cooking?" Cayenne asked.

"Stephen gave her a senior position so that she could steal from an account your father had set up for you and your sister. Under Stephen's instruction, she targeted your account in particular. Alex forged your signature, pretended to be you in documents, and stole chunks of money from the account."

"What?" Cayenne looked stunned. "I can't believe it. How could they do this? How could Alex do this to me?"

Dirk sighed, running a hand through his hair. "They were meticulous. Alex used her closeness to you to access all the right documents, and Stephen used his position as managing director to cover up any discrepancies."

"I can't believe this; it feels like a knife in the back." Tears rose in Cayenne's eyes, and she looked away, trying to process everything. "So, what now? What happens to Alex and Stephen?"

"They're already being investigated by the white-collar task force. I thought the company would have kept it hush hush, but it seems they will make an example of Stephen in particular," Dirk said. "I've gathered enough evidence to ensure they'll face serious charges. Your account should be restored soon; you will get back what's rightfully yours. I assume members of the LAD Wealth board to the lawyer, Michael Beckett, who was tricked into signing papers releasing the funds will be calling you soon to apologize. It was a lot of money."

"It was?" Cayenne frowned, "imagine that. I had no knowledge of it."

"And that's why it was easy to steal it from you," Dirk shrugged. "Alex knew how you felt toward your dad. They were almost sure they could get away with it."

"Well, thank you, Dirk. I don't know what to say." Cayenne sniffed.

"You don't have to say anything," Dirk replied gently. "I understand how tough this must be for you."

Cayenne took a deep breath, meeting his eyes. "It's a lot to take in, but I appreciate everything you've done. I am sort of in shock right now. I can't believe this of Alex."

"Do you want me to leave so that you can digest it all?" Dirk asked.

"No," Cayenne snorted. "Stay and take my mind off it, and tell me every minute detail about yourself and what you've been up to these last couple of years."

They ended up talking way into the night.

"I might have to fly out this weekend," Dirk said when he was leaving. "This is not goodbye, Cayenne, I'll leave all my numbers. We'll keep in touch, okay?"

Cayenne nodded wanly. "I just found you again."

"I think this is our time," Dirk kissed her briefly before he left. "We'll make it work."

****

He did indeed leave that weekend, and Cayenne felt inexplicably bereft. All week, she had been bombarded with calls, especially from Michael Beckett.

"We can sue," he said sternly. "LAD Wealth dropped the ball."

"I don't want that," Cayenne said. "Honestly, I am more disappointed in Alex's actions than losing money I didn't even know I had."

She tried to call Alex but didn't get a response.

Sanya woke her up on Sunday morning, squealing in her ear. "Have you seen the papers?"

"No," Cayenne said glumly, "what time is it?"

"Early. I am selling my car and I wanted to see my ad in the classifieds."

"What's in the paper?"

"Headline news," Sanya said, "Stephen Grant and Alexandria Hall, both of LAD Wealth Management, are released from their positions effective immediately. The article didn't go into much detail but mentioned a major scandal involving client funds."

"Oh my," Cayenne said.

"You don't sound surprised," Sanya was disappointed at her lackluster response.

"That's because I expected it. I had a long conversation with Dirk."

"And he told you that he was really Lance?" Sanya asked.

"Yes," Cayenne said. "How did you know?"

"I figured it out," Sanya said, "I also worked out that he was at the house that weekend in undercover mode. I was going to tell you, and then Alex spazzed out, and we left. How is he, by the way? Is he still pretending that your fake parts are not a problem?"

Cayenne chuckled. "I don't have fake parts, Sanya. Alex was wrong."

"Oh, bless!" Sanya laughed, "I am so happy for that."

"And Dirk is not here; he had to go to New York to do business. We text each other, but he is working on a sticky case that is taking up most of his time, so I don't know where we stand."

"You know where you stand," Sanya snorted, "he likes you. I have no doubt he'll come charging back here under some pretense or another. You'll have a whirlwind romance and then marriage.

"I can't believe you will get married before me, and I've been dating Caleb for four years. I like a man who knows what he wants. In my experience, if a guy loves you, he won't waste any time. He won't make excuses; he'll want to be tied to you like a puppy on steroids. I get that vibe from Dirk."

"Who said anything about marriage?" Cayenne asked.

"Let's see," Sanya mused, "the guy only had eyes for you

on the weekend. He said he would date you even if you were damaged down below. He genuinely likes you. I warned him not to hurt you, and he said he did not intend to."

"He said that?" Cayenne was suddenly awake and alert.

"Yep," Sanya said, "Mark my words, Dirk James means business, and I am not talking the numbers and ledger kind of business."

Chapter Twenty

Dirk had been in New York for six weeks but was itching to return to Jamaica. It didn't take a genius to figure out that he missed Cayenne. It was funny; she hadn't been in his life for years, and now, meeting her again, he felt a Cayenne-sized hole in his heart.

His grandfather had called him to a meeting; he had sounded somber. They had just worked on a case that had taken all the firm's manpower to solve, and everybody was exhilarated but exhausted. He knocked on his grandfather's door.

"Come on in," Simon said gruffly. He was sitting in his chair, looking at the city skyline. Dirk sat across from him.

"You know what my dream has always been?" Simon asked Dirk.

"To live in the Jamaican countryside and fuss around with your garden?" Dirk raised an eyebrow.

"Yes," Simon chuckled, "but my other dream was to start

a branch of this business in Jamaica."

"Ah," Dirk nodded.

"Today, I was negotiating with a friend of mine, Russell. He has an accounting firm he is selling out. He bought a boat; he said he wants to go sailing."

"And you were thinking of joining him?" Dirk asked.

"No," Simon said, "I was thinking of buying him out. I would work part-time at the office to keep the old brain sharp, but I would still have my garden to putter around in. Your grandmother goes home so frequently now; she is hardly here. I want to join her permanently."

"Good for you, Grandpa," Dirk said.

"But I would want someone to run it, a man of my own choosing, with whom I can share the profits fifty/fifty. Someone who recently went to Jamaica and made waves."

"You are talking about me?" Dirk asked.

"Yes," Simon nodded. "Would you be willing to head our Jamaican branch? Don't feel obligated to answer now; I understand that…"

"Yes," Dirk said without pause.

Simon chuckled. "That was fast."

"But it makes sense," Dirk said, "here I am just an employee. There, I will be in charge."

"Your aunt Pamella is going to be mad at me," Simon said. "She thinks you are the best at what you do."

"Pamella will get over it," Dirk grinned. "Besides, it's not like I'll be gone forever. I'll come back to visit, and who knows? Maybe she'll want to expand even further after seeing how successful the Jamaican branch is."

Simon nodded thoughtfully. "That's a good point. And you're right; this is an opportunity for you to grow."

Dirk leaned forward, excitement shining in his eyes. "When do we start planning?"

Simon smiled, feeling a surge of pride. "Right away. We'll need to coordinate with Russell, finalize the sale, and start setting up the office. And, of course, we'll have to plan your move."

Dirk stood up, his enthusiasm contagious. "Let's do it, Grandpa. I can't wait to get started."

Simon rose as well, extending his hand. "To new beginnings," he said.

"To new beginnings," Dirk echoed, firmly shaking his grandfather's hand.

****

"So, how are things going with you and Dirk?" Sanya asked, trying to look over her shoulders at Cayenne's phone. Cayenne paused to answer a text and smiled smugly.

Sanya was spending the weekend at Cayenne's to get her hair braided. They were sitting in the living room, watching television and chatting. Cayenne was on the last quadrant of her hair.

"Fine. Great. He just texted me and said, can't wait to see you," Cayenne answered. "We talk every day, except for this weekend; he said he was traveling. It has been a long three months."

"Oh my, traveling," Sage snorted. She was sitting beside the window, sorting through the mail. "I guess that means you guys only talk like once or twice. Usually, you can hear them whispering and giggling like teenagers. He is her new Alex. Her bestie."

"Speaking of Alex," Sanya said, "I heard she is not going to jail. She agreed to testify against Stephen but was required to pay back all the money she had acquired through the fraud. And wouldn't you know it, her crusty brother actually made some real money through his currency trading and paid it all back for her."

"That's great!" Cayenne looked up.

"She's one fortunate girl," Sanya said. "She can't work in any private sector financial institution in Jamaica again, but she got a job in government, and she didn't have to move in with her parents; her crusty brother bought a new apartment for her, and she doesn't have to sell her car either…"

"You got a new car," Cayenne said. "Let Alex and her car go. And you have to stop calling Sebastian crusty. He is obviously doing well now. I guess he is bathing regularly, too, with not a crust in sight."

"I know, I know," Sanya sighed, "but some people always land on their feet, I tell you. Speaking of my new car. I still don't understand how I got it. I supposedly won it in a supermarket lottery but never signed up for those things. And how did it arrive on my birthday?"

"A coincidence?" Cayenne raised her eyebrow. "Stop looking a gift horse in the mouth."

"And how is it the same car that I have been harping on for the last year and the same color?" Sanya shook her head. "It's puzzling."

"The Lord works in mysterious ways?" Cayenne said.

"Yes, but in this case, I think you were the one working in mysterious ways," Sanya looked at her. "Did I tell you thank you?"

"A million times," Cayenne said, "and I have not confirmed or denied that it was me. But if I were the one who did it, I would be tired of the thanks by now. I would tell you to enjoy your gift, or I may reconsider paying off your student loans as a Christmas gift."

Sanya chuckled. "You are a good friend, the best."

"She is," Sage chimed in, "she called LAD Wealth and

told them to go easy on Alex. She told them she would absorb Alex's share of the withdrawals. But Alex's brother came through before."

"You did that?" Sanya said. "Oh, Cayenne, you are better than me. I would have relished her going to jail. She used you, committed fraud, stole from you…"

"She made a mistake, a horrific and awful mistake, and while I don't think we will ever be close again, I did not want her in prison," Cayenne shrugged. "Besides, this was money I didn't even know I had. It was hard to get passionate over it."

"Oh, look here," Sage said, "it's a personal letter addressed to you, Cayenne, and one to me."

"Who is it from?" Cayenne asked.

"Paul Aubry," Sage breathed. "It's from a St. Ann address."

"I guess he is out of prison," Cayenne said, "read mine out loud."

"You sure you want me to hear this?" Sanya said.

"Sure," Cayenne nodded.

Sage opened the letter and read:

"Dear Cayenne,

I won't attempt to see you. You can put your mind at ease. Through the years, I have gotten regular updates on your progress, and I am happy to know that the short time I was in your life did not leave any lasting damage. I never harmed you in any way, Cayenne.

I did, however, harm several other children, and I am not angry that your mother colluded with Dr. Douglas to put me away. In fact, I welcomed it. I would have hurt you had I stayed in your life.

Contrary to what you have heard all your life, I am not a monster. I am mentally ill, and I should have sought help.

But I didn't, and for that, I am deeply sorry to all the children I have hurt.

I understand if you never want to forgive me, and I respect whatever decision you make. I just wanted you to know that I have always loved you in my own broken way. I hope you find peace and happiness in your life, Cayenne. You deserve nothing but the best. If you ever need anything, please don't hesitate to reach out.

With love and regret,
Your father, Paul.

"Oh dear," Cayenne said, blinking away tears.

"Yep," Sage said hoarsely. "Let me read mine." She read silently. "It's basically the same thing. Should we write him back?"

"And say what?" Cayenne asked. "Next thing you know, we are corresponding with a pedophile, and then we develop a relationship with him, and we slowly start letting him back into our lives thinking he is cured, and then we have children, and then you find him naked with one of them and then what, Sage?"

"Okay," Sage said, "I get your point."

"Give him a wide berth," Cayenne said resolutely. "I really hope they have someone watching him back in St. Ann. And just in case your resolve weakens, read the court script about what he supposedly did to me. It actually happened to another little girl. Remember that."

Sage sighed and then looked through the window. "There is a moving van next door."

"Uh-huh," Cayenne said. "That's to be expected; someone bought Mr. Henry's townhouse. They have been renovating it all month. I wanted to buy it, but it was gone by the time I decided to make my move."

"I wonder if the new neighbor is cute," Sage said.

"Don't you have a boyfriend?" Sanya asked.

"Yep, but I am thinking of breaking up with him. I have a thing for his father," Sage murmured.

Sanya laughed. "That sounds intriguing. And here I was thinking of the three spices; you were the boring one. What's the age gap like with the father?"

"Eighteen years," Sage said. "He is just thirty-nine."

"Ick," Sanya shuddered.

"My mother and father were twenty-four years apart," Sage said.

"Double ick," Sanya grimaced. "And look how that turned out."

"Bruce is not like my dad," Sage said, "far from it. I am not justifying my feelings about him to you or anyone else. I am over twenty-one."

"She told you!" Cayenne snickered.

Sanya laughed. "Yes, she did."

"Oh my," Sage whistled, pulling the curtain. "Stop the presses. The new neighbor is indeed fine."

"Describe him," Cayenne said. "Maybe today is Sanya's lucky day."

"Are you sure you don't want to come over here and see him for yourself?" Sage asked.

"Quite sure," Cayenne snorted. "Besides, I have one braid before I finish Sanya's head."

"Okay," Sage shrugged. "He is tall, about six feet tall, probably 6'1. He's brown, about the same shade as my heavenly honey foundation, and he's built like a runner."

"Long-distance or sprints?" Cayenne asked lazily.

"Sprints," Sage said.

"What's he wearing?" Cayenne finished Sanya's hair with

a flourish.

"Blue jeans. They fit perfectly. He has a slight bow in his leg."

Cayenne frowned. "Why does this description sound familiar? Do you describe all the men moving in next door the same way? That's exactly how you described Dirk the first time he was moving in."

"Maybe I am a broken record," Sage grinned. "I might need to return to school and take description classes."

"What's he wearing?" Cayenne asked.

"A white T-shirt. It has writing on it," Sage answered promptly.

"What does it say?" Cayenne stilled. "You know, I always say you can tell a man's personality by the writing on his T-shirt."

"It says I love Cayenne, and there's a heart underneath it," Sage murmured. "It has a capital C, too; how corny. Look at that, he is heading to our door."

"Dirk!" Cayenne squealed.

"Thank God she finished my hair," Sanya muttered.

Cayenne yanked the door open before Dirk could knock. "I've missed you!"

"I've missed you too," Dirk said solemnly.

He took a step closer, and she could feel the warmth of his body. Their eyes locked, and the world around them seemed to fade away. Slowly, he leaned in, and their lips met in a kiss that sent a jolt of electricity through both of them.

It was as if the connection they had always felt was suddenly magnified, an undeniable force drawing them together. The kiss deepened, and for a moment, they lost themselves in the experience.

When they finally pulled away, breathless and smiling, Dirk cupped her face in his hands. "I'm so glad to be back," he whispered.

"Me too," Cayenne replied, her eyes shining with happiness.

"And I will be your neighbor for the foreseeable future."

"You will?" Cayenne whispered.

"Yes, I bought the house from Mr. Henry. I would ask you to move in with me," Dirk said, "but I am thinking I want something a bit more permanent, like marriage."

Cayenne's eyes widened, and she felt her heart skip a beat. "Marriage?" she echoed, almost in disbelief.

Dirk nodded, his expression earnest and filled with hope. "Yes, marriage. I've thought about this a lot while I was away. I don't want to waste any more time. You mean everything to me, Cayenne."

Cayenne felt a rush of emotions—joy, surprise, love—all swirling within her. "Yes," she whispered, then louder, "Yes! I want to marry you, Dirk."

Dirk's face broke into a broad smile, and he pulled her into a tight embrace. They stood there, wrapped in each other's arms, savoring the moment.

Sage and Sanya, who had been listening, exchanged delighted glances.

"Looks like we'll be planning a wedding soon," Sanya said with a grin.

"I wholeheartedly approve," Sage added, giving Cayenne a thumbs-up.

Cayenne laughed, her happiness overflowing. "I can't believe this is happening."

"Believe it," Dirk said softly, pressing his forehead against hers. "Our future starts now."

As they shared another kiss, Cayenne knew this was just the beginning of their beautiful journey together.

The End

Thank you for reading!

Continue reading for an excerpt from Sage, the final book in the series.

Sage (Book Three Spice and Stone Series)

"Sage, can you come to my office, please?" Bruce Whitlock said briskly over the phone.

Sage jumped to attention guiltily. She had not been productive. Instead of working for Whitlock Landscaping, she was trading wedding dress ideas with her sister.

Cayenne and Dirk were having a wedding ceremony on the jetty at Sea Glass Villas, and the bride was conflicted about how sophisticated or simple her dress should be. It had turned into a family chat. Even her grandmother, Rosemary, was involved. They were all going to meet at a custom dress designer this evening at six. Sage liked a halter-neck, fishtail style that looked elegant and simple. She was so in love with the design that she pushed it on Cayenne as if it were a life-or-death matter.

She only realized that she had accidentally grabbed the bridal magazine with her laptop when she was at the door to Bruce's office. She groaned inwardly. Brian proposed every other week these days, and she didn't want to give Bruce the impression that she had weddings on the brain or was thinking about marrying his son.

In fact, for the past six months, she had been trying to break up with Brian. It was just so hard to do with him away at school. He was doing his master's in engineering at Caltech, and he had returned home twice since then. Both times when she brought up the matter, he completely ignored her efforts to break up with him. He could be so frustrating.

She gritted her teeth. The last time he was here, three months ago, she had been as brutal as possible. "Brian, I simply don't love you. I don't think we are compatible."

His response had been to laugh as if she were joking. "Sage, you're just stressed. We've been together for so long;

you probably can't imagine life without me. But trust me, it's just a phase you'll get over."

That dismissive attitude had left her seething for weeks. She had tried to give him space, hoping he'd realize the truth, but instead, he seemed more determined than ever to hold on to her. Sage was at her wit's end.

As she approached Bruce Whitlock's office, she took a deep breath and tried to compose herself. Bruce was not a man to be kept waiting, and she had already wasted enough time today. She knocked on the door, clutching her laptop and the bridal magazine.

"Come in," Bruce's voice boomed from inside.

Sage pushed the door open and stepped in, trying to hide the magazine under the laptop. Bruce looked better every time she saw him. He was the definition of tall, dark, and handsome. He had chiseled features, a strong jawline, and piercing honey-colored brown eyes that seemed to see right through her.

Today, he wore a muscle-fit black shirt that accentuated his broad shoulders and lean physique, along with his typical blue jeans. He looked good in everything.

He wasn't at the office much. He was usually supervising the larger projects or in the vast greenhouses behind the offices. Whitlock Landscaping supplied its own trees, flowers, and shrubs, so it had to stock a wide variety of plants.

Bruce didn't like being shackled to a desk.

He usually had a weekly one-on-one meeting with the small office staff to inquire about their progress. He liked getting results. As a social media manager, Cayenne usually urged customers to say where they found out about the business. So far, they had gotten some major referrals through her efforts, and she figured she was now a valuable member of the team.

He smiled at her. "Sage, have a seat."

She hurriedly sat. She had to train herself not to swoon when he smiled. One would think that after dating his son for two years and seeing Bruce every week, she would be able to resist that smile, but it still made her weak in the knees. He had no idea how she felt. She would be mortified if he did.

"So, I was commissioned to do a multimillion-dollar project," Bruce leaned forward. "It is an all-inclusive golf resort. The property developers want us to design a large golf course and landscape the entire property, including luxury gardens, walking paths, and multiple themed areas. It's a huge opportunity for Whitlock Landscaping, and it's largely because of the exceptional work you've done marketing us. You deserve every dime I pay you and more."

Sage smiled. "I am glad I am making a difference here at Whitlock Landscaping."

"We could do a series on this project for social media," Bruce said. "The villas are not yet done, but that's okay. The client wants us to start working on the gardens of the newly renovated family house on the other side of the resort. It will remain a private property and will overlook the golf course."

"Oh wow," Sage nodded. "It sounds pretty, and yes, a series would be a great idea. I could record you and then edit the videos from the beginning to the final reveal. That's actually an excellent idea."

Bruce nodded. "I am curious to know if you know the property developer. He shares the same last name as you."

"I am not sure," Sage said. "What's his name?"

"Horace Aubry, the house being renovated is Aubry House."

"Er," Sage was stunned. "I don't know Horace. I have heard of him. He is my father's younger brother. And I didn't know they had a place called Aubry House."

"Oh, your father," Bruce frowned. "I know all about your father. Will this be a problem? Because if it is, we can call this off."

"Oh no," Sage said. "I would never ask you to do that. I don't know Horace, and maybe he doesn't know me. I don't see why this should change anything."

Bruce smiled. "Very well. I'll work on the design for the house grounds. It's three acres on a hill; it should be fun."

Sage chuckled. "I'll need footage of that, your drawings, and the property. I need some good before shots."

Bruce nodded. "Yes. We start working on Monday. I hope you don't mind staying over at my farm in St. Ann, at least on weekdays. It would be easier for the men and me not to drive to and from Kingston daily. The men will bunk in the farmhouses. You will stay with me at the main house."

Sage swallowed. Staying with him? Why did that sound so intimate, and why was she so excited about the prospect?

"Well, er, I have no problem at all," Sage said.

Bruce's eyes twinkled with amusement. "Good to know," he said, leaning back in his chair. "I promise you'll have all the amenities you need."

Sage nodded, trying to suppress the butterflies in her stomach. "Sounds great."

Bruce's phone buzzed on the table as they settled the final details. He glanced at the screen and frowned slightly. "Excuse me for a moment," he said, standing up and stepping away to take the call.

Sage took a deep breath, allowing herself a moment to absorb everything. Working with Bruce on such a personal project was thrilling, not just because of the professional opportunity but also because of the undeniable chemistry she felt between them. She pushed the thought aside. Focus on the job, she reminded herself.

When Bruce returned, his expression had softened. "Everything's all set then. I'll see you on Monday, Sage."

"Looking forward to it," she replied, standing up to shake his hand. His grip was firm, and for a moment, he held her gaze, making her heart race and her skin tingle where he touched her.

The bridal magazine chose that moment to drop from her nerveless fingers.

He glanced at it and then at her. "I didn't know you and Brian were that serious."

"We aren't," Sage cleared her throat. "Well, I am not serious. What I mean to say is... it's for my sister's wedding."

Bruce raised an eyebrow, a flicker of amusement dancing in his eyes. "Your sister's wedding, huh? Well, that makes more sense."

Sage could feel the heat rising to her cheeks. "Yes, she's getting married in a few months. I'm just helping her out with some ideas."

Bruce nodded, a playful smile curling at the corners of his mouth. "Got it. If you need any tips on venues or anything, let me know. I might know a thing or two about making places look beautiful."

Sage laughed, the tension easing. "We might just take you up on that."

"Great," Bruce said, his tone light but his gaze steady. "So, Monday it is. We'll get started on the house grounds and see where the week takes us."

"Monday," Sage echoed.

She couldn't wait for Monday. Why wasn't it Monday yet? Anticipation sliced through her as she walked out of his office. What would it be like working so closely with Bruce? Would she reveal her feelings for him, or would she keep her composure?

Discover Exclusive Offers and Be the First to Know!

If you haven't already, don't miss out on the opportunity to join my New Release Newsletter! Sign up today and become part of an exclusive community where you'll be among the first to hear about my latest book releases and take advantage of special prices.

Why join my mailing list?

Be the First: Get a head start and be the first to know when I release a new book.

Exclusive Discounts: Unlock special prices available only to subscribers. Enjoy limited time offers and save big on your favorite books.

Quick and Easy: Signing up takes less than 30 seconds.

To join, visit https://www.brenalbar.com/newsletter or scan the QR code below.

Thank you for your support, and happy reading!

Ridgeview Series

The Ridgeview series follows five couples on the Jamaican north coast in the luxurious community of Ridgeview. It explores their everyday struggles with careers, children, and family drama. Each book touches on love, marriage, and trust as the characters face challenges that test their relationships.

Ride or Die (Book 1)
Play For Keeps (Book 2)
Through Thick and Thin (Book 3)
Tried and True (Book 4)
Stay With You (Book 5)

Spice and Stone Series

Join three extraordinary girls—Cinnamon, Cayenne, and Sage— as they navigate the intricate flavors of life, love, and romance in the captivating Spice and Stone series.

Cinnamon (Book 1)
Cayenne (Book 2)
Sage (Book3)

The Crimson Hill Series

Where family drama, romance, and a touch of sci-fi blend seamlessly in the enchanting backdrop of a small town in Jamaica. Prepare to embark on an unforgettable journey as secrets unravel, passions ignite, and destinies intertwine.

No Goodbye (Book 1)
No Misunderstanding (Book 2)
No Ordinary Love (Book 3)
No Fairy Tale (Book 4)
No Letting Go (Book 5)
No Strings Attached (Book 6)
No More Mrs. Nice Girl (Book 7)
No Place Like You (Book 8)
Knight and Day (Book 8.5)
No Expectations (Book 9)
Ice and Fyre (Book 9.5)
No Surrender (Book 10)
No Time for Love (Book 11)
No Promises (Book 12)
Winter's Eve (Book 13)

The Wiley Brothers

Step into the world of the Wiley Brothers, where tragedy weaves an unbreakable bond and love becomes their guiding light. In this captivating series, follow the journey of six remarkable boys as they navigate the tumultuous path of growing up without parents, discovering love, and finding their place in a challenging world.

Between Brothers (Book 0)- How it all began…
For Pete's Sake (Book 1)- Preston's story.
Crossing Jordan (Book 2)-Jordan's story.
Fire and Walter (Book 3)- Walter's story.
The Perfect Guy (Book 4)-Guy's Story.
The Patience of a Saint (Book 5)- Saint's Story.
A Case of Love (Book 6)- Case's Story.

The Pryce Sisters

Follow the remarkable journey of the Pryce triplets as they navigate the complexities of growing up, discovering romance, and embracing the exhilarating challenges of the new adult years.

Baby For A Pryce- Book 1
Right Pryce Wrong Time – Book 2
Yours, For A Pryce- Book 3

The Jacksons

Prepare to be enthralled by the captivating saga of the Jackson family. In this gripping series, secrets unravel, paternity questions loom, and love blooms in the most unexpected corners.

Ace- Book 1
Deuce- Book 2
Trey- Book 3
Quade- Book 4

The Scarlett Series

Their patriarch died and unexpectedly left each of them a fortune. Watch as the Scarlett family navigate their way through the ups and downs of sudden wealth, family secrets, and the complicated dynamics of their relationships.

Scarlett Baby (Book 1)
Scarlett Sinner (Book 2)
Scarlett Secret (Book 3)
Scarlett Love (Book 4)
Scarlett Promise (Book 5)
Scarlett Bride (Book 6)
Scarlett Heart (Book 7)

Magnolia Sisters

They were the rejects. The worst of the lot, they grew up in a girl's home together and formed sisterly bonds. Each book in the series tells the story of a different girl and the unique struggles and triumphs she faces along the way. With themes of friendship, forgiveness, and the power of love, the "Magnolia Sisters" series is a heartwarming and inspiring read that you won't want to put down.

Dear Mystery Guy- Book 1
Bad Girl Blues- Book 2
Her Mistaken Dream- Book 3
Just Like Yesterday – Book 4

New Song Series

A group of friends started out as a church band, see how each of them navigate their personal and professional lives while staying true to their faith and facing challenges along the way. With themes of forgiveness, redemption, and second chances, the New Song Series is a captivating read for anyone who enjoys heartwarming stories of love and faith.

Going Solo- Book 1
Duet on Fire- Book 2
Tangled Chords- Book 3
Broken Harmony- Book 4
A Past Refrain- Book 5
Perfect Melody- Book 6

The Bancrofts

The Bancroft family delves into the inner workings of academia and the high-stakes world of university politics. The family wrestles with the pressures of maintaining their family's legacy, they must confront their own demons and navigate the complex relationships that bind them together. From unexpected love affairs and betrayals to scandals and secrets that threaten to tear them apart, this is a series that will keep you captivated until the very end.

Homely Girl- Book 0
Saving Face- Book 1
Tattered Tiara- Book 2
Private Dancer- Book 3
Goodbye Lonely- Book 4
Practice Run- Book 5
Sense of Rumor- Book 6
A Younger Man- Book 7
Just To See Her- Book 8

Three Rivers Series

Three Rivers Series, a captivating tale of love, redemption, and second chances set in a picturesque community in St. Ann's Bay, Jamaica.

Private Sins- Book 1
Loving Mr. Wright- Book 2
Unholy Matrimony- Book 3
If It Ain't Broke- Book 4

The Resetter Series

The Resetter Series takes a look at a rare kind of person, a person who can travel back in time, but they only have one chance to get things right if they go back! With themes of second chances, changing the past and the power of love, the resetters series is a captivating time travel romance that many readers have described as a page turner.

Never Too Late- Book 1
Never Say Never- Book 2
Now or Never- Book 3
Almost Never- Book 4

On the Rebound Series

Experience the gripping and emotionally charged On the Rebound series, where love, betrayal, and redemption collide in a whirlwind of passion and secrets. Brace yourself for a journey filled with drama, cheating scandals, DNA questions, and ultimately, the power of second chances and finding love again.

On the Rebound- Book 1
On the Rebound Book 2

Standalone Books

Full Circle- After graduating from university, Diana wanted to return to Jamaica to find her siblings. What she didn't foresee was that she would meet Robert Cassidy and that both their pasts would be intertwined, and that disturbing questions would pop up about their parentage just when they were getting close.

After the End- Torn between two lovers. Colleen married her high school sweetheart, Isaiah, hoping that they would live happily ever after, but life intruded, and Isaiah disappeared at sea. She found work with the rich and handsome Enrique Lopez as a housekeeper and realized that she couldn't keep him at arm's length.

Love Triangle: Three Sides to the Story- George, the husband. Marie, the wife, and Karen-the mistress. They all get to tell their side of the story.

New Beginnings- Inner-city girl Geneva was offered an opportunity of a lifetime when she learned that her 'real' father was a wealthy man. Her decision to live up-town meant she had to leave Froggie, her 'ghetto don,' behind. She also found herself battling with her stepmother and battling her emotions for Justin, a suave up-towner.

The Preacher and the Prostitute- Prostitution and the clergy don't mix. Tell that to ex-prostitute Maribel, who finds herself in love with the Pastor at her church. Can an ex-prostitute and a pastor have a future together?

Historical Fiction

You won't want to miss out on these two captivating reads!

"The Pull of Freedom" tells the story of a slave family and their desperate struggle for freedom in Jamaica's colonial era. Follow the journey of these brave individuals as they fight for their right to be free, facing danger, heartbreak, and unimaginable obstacles along the way.

"The Empty Hammock" takes readers on a journey through time, as a modern woman finds herself transported back to the Taino era of Jamaica's history. Experience the wonder and mystery of this ancient culture through her eyes, as she learns about their traditions, beliefs, and way of life. With richly drawn characters and a beautifully realized setting, "The Empty Hammock" is a must-read for anyone who loves historical fiction that transports them to another time and place.

Short Story Collections

Di Taxi Ride and Other Stories- Funny stories about Jamaican life to make you laugh.

www.ingramcontent.com/pod-product-compliance
Lightning Source LLC
Chambersburg PA
CBHW050520160726
48003CB00001B/390